The Man, The Myth, The Legend

The Man, The Myth, The Legend

SHORT STORIES

CHRIS ORCUTT

The Man, The Myth, The Legend

A Collection of Short Stories
by Chris Orcutt

Third Print Edition: 2018

This is a work of fiction. Names, characters, places, and incidents either are the product of the author's imagination or are used fictitiously. Any resemblance to actual persons (living or dead), companies, institutions, events or locales is entirely coincidental and not intended by the author. Most of the characters in "The Magnificent Murphy" are taken from F. Scott Fitzgerald's The Great Gatsby; the author wishes to acknowledge Fitzgerald's brilliant novel as the inspiration for his modest spoof.

ISBN-13: 978-0692205402 (Have Pen, Will Travel)

The cover artist for this book is Elisabeth Pinio, a graphic designer based in the Silicon Valley. The photograph on the cover, "315/365 - The 365 Toy Project," is by David D. (a.k.a. puuikibeach) on Flickr; the photo is of a Hasbro Inc. Indiana Jones action figure. The ebook formatter is EBook Converting|High Quality Ebook Conversion: ebookconverting.com

Also by Chris Orcutt:

A Real Piece of Work (Dakota Stevens Mystery #1)
The Rich Are Different (Dakota Stevens Mystery #2)
A Truth Stranger Than Fiction (Dakota Stevens Mystery #3)
One Hundred Miles from Manhattan (A Novel)

www.orcutt.net

For Joseph Kubancik,
an ardent fan of these stories
and the rarest of men:
A kind father-in-law,
A loving father,
An honest lawyer,
And a good human being.
Before you fade into the cornfield,
know that you will be remembered.
Thank you, Joe.

CONTENTS

THE LAST GREAT WHITE HUNTER

His name was Buck Remington, and with a name like that he was destined to become one of the greatest Great White Hunters in Africa. Among his female clients he was known by another name, but how Buck earned that moniker is the subject of an infamous unauthorized biography and will not be discussed here.

So, what kind of a man was he? More than a man's man, that's for sure.

He was a man's man's man.

Stronger and more virile than a dozen of today's video game-playing punks, even at age 85 when he undertook his last safari Buck Remington made Clint Eastwood and Anthony Quinn look like towel boys in a Turkish bathhouse. He never lost a bar fight or a poetry quoting or drinking contest. Nairobi swam in his illegitimate offspring—the sons and daughters of cooks and seamstresses, heiresses and plantation owners. As for his own history, it was as though he'd been born in the savanna and raised by lions. He spoke a polyglot of American and British English, with a smattering of Swahili picked up in the bush, leading some to believe he was the orphaned son of an American industrialist or, like Tarzan, the descendant of a long-lost member of the Peerage. In the

1980s there was talk of his being knighted, but when neither Buck's birthplace nor his citizenship could be proved, the matter was quietly dropped.

His long and storied career began when he was but 9 years old (he looked 16) as an assistant to legendary English hunter Philip Percival, on the maiden safari of American writer Ernest Hemingway. Observing Buck's innate, highly developed skills of tracking and shooting, and his extraordinary "grace under pressure," as Hemingway called it, both men predicted a bright future for the boy hunter.

To lesser men, Buck's 76-year career had been a smashing success, but his accomplishments were not enough to douse the fires of ambition that burned hotter in him than a South African dry season. In fact he considered himself a jackal of a failure, having bagged only 162 rhino, 217 elephant, 496 lion, 375 Bengal tiger, 306 antelope (fast buggers), 285 cheetah, 609 Cape buffalo, 531 kudu, 439 leopard, countless hyena (stopped counting after 900), 55 crocodiles, 16 hippo (self-defense), a savage thieving baboon, and a handful of wild dogs, shot for practice from a moving truck.

It was reflecting on these paltry numbers that caused Buck Remington to rise from bed more slowly than usual on the morning of his final safari. His bedmate was an American divorcee who had been inspired to travel the world after reading that *Eat, Pray, Love* bollocks. He slapped her backside.

"Time to go, my dear."

"One more time, Buck. Please?"

"Sorry, love. Meet my clients in three-quarters of an hour, and I haven't breakfasted yet. Breakfast for one, I'm afraid."

He called downstairs and ordered his usual be brought up. The door clicked shut when the woman left. He retrieved his revolver, a Freedom Arms Model 83, from beneath the pillow and holstered it. Chambered for .475 Linebaugh, it made a .44 magnum seem like a child's cap gun. It could stop a charging lion dead at 20 feet and had deterred more than a few jealous husbands.

Buck was at the sink, shaving with the straight razor he had once used to cut a lion's throat, when breakfast arrived: steak & eggs, toast with marmalade, a pot of black Kenyan coffee, and a very stiff Bloody Mary (one needed one's vegetables). He sawed into the rare beef, sipped the coffee, quaffed the hair of the dog. His houseboy entered with his jacket and hat.

"Lucky jacket, Bwana."

"Good. Hang it up there."

Buck finished his breakfast, checked the time and went to the bush jacket. It was the last of two dozen a client had given him long ago, back when Abercrombie & Fitch was a high-end outfitter, before they became a purveyor of snug undershirts for sexually confused teenagers. For a moment he stood in the light from the window, admiring the good stout twill, the reinforced elbows like rhino hide, the elastic loops holding the obscene cartridges for his Holland and Holland .600NE double rifle. Looked like shells for a bloody flak gun. The pockets contained the essentials: a dozen extra .475

shells, two packs of Chesterfields, matches, and a flask of Macallan 18-year.

As he removed the jacket from its hanger and slipped it on, he glanced at himself in the mirror. Freshly shaved, tanned and with his full head of hair, Buck routinely passed for a brisk man of 50 among his female clients and the patronesses of hotel bars around the world. Today, however, he didn't feel young. Today he was overcome by a sense of finality. He knew he wouldn't be coming back from this safari. How that old bastard Death would finally get him—shot in the head by his client, impaled on a rhino horn, mauled in the brush trying to finish off a wounded leopard—he had no idea. He only hoped it would be worthy of the life he'd lived as a great hunter and not something undignified, like what had happened to his old rival, Richards. A decade later, and Buck still couldn't think about it.

The private jet was taxiing in when Murubi—his all-around driver, tracker and gun-bearer—parked the Land Rover on the tarmac. Time was, clients flew in on whatever taped-together deathtrap happened to be going to Nairobi, or they came in by rail and he got his first look at them through a cloud of steam. Nowadays they arrived like deposed dictators. Billionaires, mostly. They were the only ones who could afford him and the massive bribes he'd been forced to pay the Kenyan Game Commission since 1978, when they ostensibly outlawed big-game hunting.

"S'a big one, Bwana," Murubi said.

"It is."

Much bigger than the Lears they usually arrived in. Buck wondered if the client had an ego to match.

"Let's go," he said.

The jet had stopped, its engines whining down, when he got his first look at the client. Down came the door-stairs, and ten seconds later Kendall Cameron appeared in the doorway and paused—crisp new hunting garb, massive Bowie knife, binoculars, mirrored sunglasses, and jelled blond hair that the tsetse flies were going to love. Chin erect, he strode down the stairs.

"Good morning, Mr. Cameron," Buck said. "Comfortable flight, I presume."

The man's handshake was as firm as a chicken cutlet.

"Yes, you'd think so, wouldn't you? But it was *so* long."

Buck nodded. "Hope you brought a hat."

"Oh, I'm sure there's one in there someplace." He nodded at two steamer trunks leaving the tail section. He frowned at the Rover. "This is it? For a month-long safari?"

"No," Buck said. "The crew are already at camp with the other supplies and the rest of your party."

"The Nathansons? Good. Ah, here she is."

Buck's immediate impressions of Nora Cameron, the actress-humanitarian, were that her tanned legs glittered like they'd been rolled in diamond dust, and that her smile could light up a remote landing strip on a moonless night. Her age was hard to guess, as it always was with ravishing women, but Buck put her in her early 40s—the dangerous time, as he called it. Walking down the stairs, she smiled unflinchingly at him. Normally Buck was impervious to female clients' charms, but there was a glint of joy in this one's eyes that made her far more attractive than the others with their dead, rapacious stares. Her angelic look, and the fact that on her the khaki shirt and shorts seemed like lingerie, made Buck's throat catch for an instant, carried him back to his premonition in the mirror that morning, and dredged up a feeling that went much further back, to a time he had fought all his life to forget.

She stood on her tiptoes and kissed him on the cheek. Buck hadn't been kissed so affectionately in over 65 years.

"Mr. Remington, it's an honor," she said. "You took my friend Caprice Quinn on safari a couple of years ago, and she said you—the safari, I mean—was one of the best experiences of her life."

"Caprice…yes, I remember. Wasn't keen about a woman with that name handling a gun, but she turned out to be one of the best shots I've ever worked with."

"Well, I hope I prove satisfactory to you, Mr. Remington."

"Please, my dear, call me Buck." He appraised her like he was picking a prime antelope from a herd. "You're going to do just fine. Now, shall we go? Camp is quite some distance from here."

Kendall whipped off his sunglasses. "What? You mean we're not there yet?"

"Hardly, Mr. Cameron," Buck said. "Kenya is a very large country. We've several hours to drive, and over very rough terrain, before we reach camp. Should be there in time for dinner."

"Several *hours?*"

"Come on, Kendall," Nora said. "You're paying for an adventure. This is it."

Buck made sure the trunks were securely strapped to the roof platform, and that the jerry jugs of petrol and water were full and secure as well. Satisfied, he grabbed his gun from the rack, closed the tailgate and went up front. The client was in his seat.

"Mr. Cameron, I'll need you to sit in back with your wife."

"But I get car sick in back."

Behind Mr. Cameron, Murubi grinned and shook his head. Buck had dealt with this man's type before. He simply stood still with the .600 crooked in his arm, and eventually, like a child, the man got tired of waiting and quietly moved to the back.

It was after dinner, and while his two understudies, Harris and Simba, worked with the crew preparing for the first day, Buck sat around the campfire with the clients and their guests, the Nathansons, drinking some fine Plymouth gin Nora had brought.

"Excellent dinner, Buck," Nora said.

"Yes, quite," Mr. Nathanson said.

"Wonderful," his wife added. "What was that bird again?"

"Guinea fowl," Buck said. "The boys took a dozen before we arrived. It's a staple out here, so get used to it."

"It's so gamey, though," Kendall said.

Buck took a long swallow of gin. The entire drive from Nairobi, all the man did was complain. *It's so hot. My God, it's dusty. I'm parched. Is there shade where we're going? Doesn't this jalopy of yours have any shocks? I'm nauseous.*

Even when Buck pointed out a pride of lions resting in the bush, and Nora oohed and aahed, the husband carped about how much smaller they looked than he'd expected. But it wasn't until Kendall got his first tsetse fly bite and the man screamed as though he'd been bitten by a black mamba that Buck realized what kind of client he was saddled with: a tenderfoot, and the worst kind at that—a goddamn pansy one.

The wife was something else entirely: cultured, optimistic, appreciative, and, unlike any other movie star he'd met, humble. And beautiful? My God. He'd bedded his share of gorgeous creatures before, but Nora radiated beauty like heat. She smiled at him across the campfire. Buck stood.

"Now that we're all here, there's a little speech I always give," he said. "It's important, so please listen. This is not New York or Los Angeles. This, in case you haven't noticed, is the middle of nowhere. Yes, it's God's country, and yes it's beautiful, but make no mistake, it's deadly. Anything out here can kill you. *Anything.* Never mind the obvious—like a lion or a snakebite—get a bad scratch from a thorn and you'll find yourself going the way of Ivan Ilyich."

The women laughed. Clearly, the men hadn't read that story of Tolstoy's.

"The point is," he continued, "stick close to me, Harris or Murubi at all times. Lastly, out here my word is law. No exceptions. I've been doing this nearly 80 years and I've never lost a client or their friends, and I plan to keep it that way. Wake-up is at four-thirty, so I suggest you all get your beauty rest. Tomorrow we'll start with zebra. Good night."

Kendall nodded and yawned. He and the Nathansons said goodnight, and then Buck was alone with Nora.

"You ought to get some sleep, too, Mrs. Cameron. You had a long day, and tomorrow's going to be even longer."

"Please, it's Nora," she said. "I will. Just enjoying my first African night. Who knew it could be so cold? Good thing we have this nice fire."

"Have to even when it's hot," Buck said.

"Lions?"

"Sure. And hyenas, leopards. Anything that moves really."

She walked around the fire, sat down on the log inches from him, and poured gin in his cup. Even drunk warm around a campfire, Plymouth Navy Strength always went down icy.

"Good gin," he said. "But I don't want to drink your whole stash."

"I heard it was your favorite, so I brought half a trunk of the stuff."

"Well then." He swilled the rest back and held out his cup for a refill. Nora's body was against his now.

"Brrr. My goodness, how do you stand it, Buck? So cold."

"My dear, that's what a warm bed is for. And it's where you need to go now. We'll both need our wits tomorrow."

"You're right." She pecked him on the cheek, put the bottle in his hand and stood up. "Get some sleep yourself, Buck."

"I shall. See you at dawn."

Buck knew what kind of day he was in for when Kendall alighted from his tent half an hour late wearing a pith helmet. Mosquito netting was draped over it like a veil and cinched to his jacket collar.

"Mr. Cameron," Buck said, "how do you expect to shoot wearing that? You won't be able to see out of the scope."

"It's fine. Damned if I'll be bitten by a tsetse fly again."

"You're sure to get bitten again, Mr. Cameron."

"Nope, not again."

Buck was about to say something cruel when Harris and Simba approached.

"Buck," Harris said, "we're taking the Nathansons out, right?"

"Yes, but they're photographers and won't be shooting. Get them close enough to take some good pictures, but I want both of you backing them up. And use the big doubles. Don't take any chances."

"Got it."

"Yes, Bwana," Simba said. "Good luck."

Murubi drove him and the Camerons to a hilly plain he'd hunted successfully many times. The sun jutted over the horizon when they arrived. Once he had gauged the wind direction, Buck led them in a long crawl to the top of a hill, where, 200 yards below, a herd of zebra grazed in the stirring grasses. The spot was one of the best he'd hunted from, and under the best conditions: uphill and downwind from the quarry, and with the sun at their backs, making it almost impossible for the notoriously skittish zebras to spot them. Murubi slid the .375 toward Buck and whispered in Swahili.

"What'd he say?" Nora asked.

"That we shan't get a better chance than this. All right, Kendall, take off that silly net and get ready to shoot."

"Why? I can see just fine."

"No you can't. It's dangerous."

With a sigh, he untied the netting and took hold of the gun.

"Okay," Buck said. "Now up on one knee. Take that one closest to us, the one away from the herd."

Buck watched him. When the man looked steady, Buck said, "Wait. Take aim behind the front shoulder, inhale, let it out and then *squeeze* the trigger. Don't yank it."

Kendall took a long time to do it. Finally, Buck whispered, "All right, bust him."

"Bust him?"

"It means *shoot*, dammit."

He turned to Buck. "Oh, don't you worry. I'll—"

The gun went off.

"Whoops," Kendall said. "Must've tightened up there."

Buck looked at the herd. Amazingly, they hadn't even flinched. It was the first time he'd ever seen a zebra herd fail to bolt at the first shot.

"You got lucky. Try again, same one. Go."

Buck watched the zebra as Kendall fired. He was too far away to hear the usual *WHAP!* as the bullet hit, but he did see the dust explode off its hide. Trouble was, the shot didn't go through the shoulder; it went in the zebra's hind leg. The herd began to stampede. Buck grabbed the .600 and took aim.

"Cover your ears!"

It was something he'd had to do a thousand times before when clients missed their targets: finish off a wounded animal. The zebra hobbled and was falling back from the herd. Buck led the animal in his sights, waited until it made a quarter-turn and was perfectly perpendicular, then unloaded on it. The zebra folded forward and skidded into the grass.

"Holy crap!" Kendall said. "And without a scope!"

"Wow. Nice shooting," Nora said.

Buck stood up. "Let's go. We need to reach the kill before the lions."

"Where's Murubi going?" Nora asked.

Buck reloaded his gun and carried it at at half-port.

"To call the skinners on the radio. Both of you follow me."

For the next week, the routine didn't vary—wake before sunrise, go on a hunt that the husband somehow botched, listen to him bitch about the bugs or the heat or the gamey food, and hear him beg to use the big gun. In the evenings they drank gin around the campfire, and—once everyone else had retired—he chatted and laughed with the lovely Nora. With each day spent in her company, Buck felt himself growing attached to her. Even if some of her conversation was uncomfortably pointed.

"You're the quintessential strong, silent type, Buck," she said. "Which leads me to wonder what deep secret you're hiding."

"Nothing. I'm as simple as they come."

She jabbed at the campfire with a stick. "I'll tell you mine," she whispered. "I don't love my husband. He gives me money and I give him status. That's it."

"If it works, it works." He poured himself more gin.

"I don't know, Buck, and you can tell me if I'm out of line, but you seem like a man who's been keeping something bottled up—something tragic—for a very long time. Why don't you tell me about it? It's good to share these things."

"Is it?"

"Yes, it is."

"That's a shame then," he said, "because there's nothing to tell, my dear."

———————◆◦◆◦◆———————

Buck had promised Mr. Cameron a male lion, but even after a week the man wasn't ready for that yet—not even close. Instead, Buck took them some miles away to an area frequented by antelope, and as they crouched behind an enormous anthill, Kendall dropped a nice male.

"How was that, Buck?"

"Better. We'll make a hunter of you yet."

Buck waved to Murubi for the skinners. It was important the animal be skinned and the meat quartered and stored before the vultures began to circle. Vultures brought the lions, and close upon their heels, the hyenas. Nora, he observed, walked close to him as they started across the open ground. The clearing was encircled by dense brush and flat-topped acacia trees—places where lions rested in the heat of the day. But the smell of fresh meat would draw them out.

"Kendall, you watch over there. Any movement, tell me. If there's a charge, drop to the ground and let me handle it."

"When do I get to shoot the big gun?"

"It's still too much gun. Be patient." Buck scanned the scrubby undergrowth for the hint of a rustling leaf. It was nearing eleven o'clock, and the air was hot and unnaturally still. "When you have some more experience with the .375, then you can try the finisher."

"Listen to Buck, dear," Nora said. "He hasn't steered you wrong yet."

Nora stood so close that Buck felt the give of her breast against his arm. Glancing at her, he was surprised by what he saw. Instead of facing him with slitted eyelids, which 9 times out of 10 signaled adulterous intentions, she anxiously studied the edge of the clearing. Like a lot of actresses, Nora had high, wonderful cheekbones one could open letters with, and when she turned to him and smiled, there was nothing coy or conspiratorial in that either.

"I'm having a great time, Buck," she said. "It's always wonderful to spend time with a master at something. You remind me a little of the Dalai Lama."

"I didn't know His Holiness liked to hunt."

She ribbed him. A puff of air drifted across the clearing. Buck thought he smelled a trace of something, but he couldn't be sure.

"I'm hardly a master," he said, "nor would I ever think of myself that way. In this business, the second you start thinking you've got all the answers, you're dead. Hold it."

He crouched in the center of the clearing. Man and wife squatted beside him. The brush was 100 yards away in each direction, and the kill, which was already gathering flies, waited 50 yards ahead.

"What is it, Buck?"

"Nothing."

The Rover and service truck droned in the distance.

"Oh, good," Nora said, "the cavalry."

"Exactly," Buck said, and before he realized it, while the husband's back was turned, he had stroked her hair.

Once the skinners had done their work, Buck put the Camerons in the Rover.

"Aren't you coming, Buck?"

"Murubi will be back for me. There's something I want to check out first."

Nora blew him a kiss as they drove off, and for some reason the playful gesture affected him more deeply than the most nude and willing woman ever had. He had the inexplicable urge to hug the little lady when he got back to camp, to brush hair from her face and caress her cheek. This feeling was so foreign to him, so confusing, it was as though a huge Bengal tiger had walked into his gun sights and Buck was unable to squeeze the trigger.

The vehicles drove out of sight and earshot. Buck stood still in the clearing. Then, seemingly out of nowhere, a dust devil swirled into the open ground, carrying with it the distinct smells of dung, mud and putrid animal flesh. The dust devil made a loop around the hard-baked earth and dissipated at the clearing edge. The smells were stronger now. Buck pulled two more Nitro Express shells for the .600 and scissored them tightly between his pinkie and ring ringer. Mr. Percival himself had taught him that. Better to have two extra shells ready, he said, because if one needed to reload quickly, the extra seconds could save one's life. And it had—many times. Buck turned in a circle, studying the brush for the faintest movement.

From behind the anthill, a male lion stepped into view and let loose with a barrage of barking roars. Branches snapped in the thicket to Buck's left, and a dark shape formed in the greenery until the snout, massive horns and perpetually angry eyes of a Cape buffalo emerged. It stopped at the cusp of the clearing and snorted. Wonderful. Two of the bastards to deal with. The buff would have to go first; it'd take two shots to finish it. He had just leveled the gun on it when a crash rose up behind him. The brush shook, a baboon squealed, branches broke. Without even seeing it yet, Buck knew it was a black rhinoceros, and then its scarred horn impaled the leaves and the beast plowed through. Like the Cape buffalo opposite, it stopped and snorted. The three animals stood dumbly where they were, as if waiting for something. In all his years of hunting, Buck had never seen anything like this. These animals shunned each other. But here they seemed to be cooperating—hunting *him*. Buck secured two more shells in his other hand. The lion concerned him, of course, but its flesh was soft and it could be brought down at very close range with one shot. He was more concerned about the buff and rhino, and after a split second's debate over which he should shoot first, he settled on the buffalo.

CHRIS ORCUTT

It had been waiting longer and was starting its agitated scuffing of the dirt; besides, however mean rhinos looked, Cape buffalo were pure malevolence: they wanted to kill you just for looking at them. Again Buck swung the gun around, and the instant his forefinger touched the trigger, squawking birds exploded out of the brush to his left. An elephant. And by the girth of its dusty gray hide, Buck judged it was a bull. And a big bull at that. It halted at the edge of the clearing. Its ivory was some of the brightest white he'd ever seen—nearly as brilliant as Nora's teeth. *Nora. Damn it, this was no time to think about her.* The elephant raised its tusks and trumpeted at him. The buggers had long memories. For all he knew, Buck might have shot his grandfather. Well, if Buck was going to die, this was how he wanted it—facing down four of Africa's deadliest animals. No sooner did he have the thought than an enormous leopard poured off a branch and crept beautifully slim and muscular into the grass near the elephant, where Buck lost sight of him. So, this is how it would end: him versus the Big Five. Behind him, the lion roared. Buck pivoted in 90° increments, gauging each animal's disposition and likelihood to charge. He didn't like the look of that damn buff, and as it wheeled to face him, Buck let loose with the .600.

He came to in his tent. His head pounded. His left shoulder burned as though a thousand Chesterfields had been extinguished on his skin. He sat up slightly. He was most definitely in his cot. Viewed through the mosquito netting, the light at the mouth of the tent had a soft haze.

There were murmuring voices outside. A breeze that was less hot, but by no means cool, stirred the tent flaps and whisked around like a liberated spirit. The stench of rotting flesh swirled in the air.

His jacket hung on a hook behind him. He had a snort from the flask, lit a cigarette, and as he blew out the match, he had the eerie sensation he was being watched. Up on his elbows on the cot, he looked askance. Not three feet away through the flimsy netting, a hyena studied him with its perpetually demonic grin. It stepped forward and licked its chops as though waiting for Buck to toss it a goddamn bone. "Cheeky bastard," Buck whispered, and with his eyes still angled uncomfortably in the animal's direction, he slid his hand under the pillow.

The gun wasn't there.

He groped around the cot. The hyena nosed closer, still grinning, showing no outward signs of aggression, but that's what made them so dangerous—people underestimated the bastards. He'd seen that same simper on their faces as they disemboweled antelope alive; he wasn't fooled for a second. This one was an old rogue by the looks of it. Must have smelled the blood and thought he'd get an easy meal.

Finally Buck's searching fingers touched smooth leather, and he continued until they hit cold steel. His revolver. Only five shots. He hoped he hadn't emptied the thing on that leopard. Couldn't remember.

Slowly, Buck pulled the gun out. The two sounds in the tent—the scratch of the gun against the holster and the panting of the hyena—seemed in a macabre race. He raised the gun and extended his arm as far as he could.

This aroused the hyena's interest. It pushed its open mouth against the mosquito netting, inching its snout closer and closer to Buck's ribs.

Buck pulled the trigger. In the confined space of the tent, the report was deafening. The shot went right through the hyena's opening jaws and took the back of its head off. It crumpled to the tent floor, twitched for an instant, and was still.

Simba entered the tent with Harris right behind him. They saw the dead hyena.

"Jeez, Buck," Harris said, "where'd he come from?"

"Bwana all right?" Simba asked.

"I'm fine." Buck threw his legs off the cot. "Toss me that bottle of gin."

When he'd had a good long pull, he reloaded the pistol.

"Buck, what happened?"

It was Nora, peeking into the tent. The setting sun cast a halo around her head. She grimaced as Harris and Simba dragged the carcass outside.

"Spot of trouble with a hyena," Buck said. "Nothing to worry about, my dear."

She kneeled beside the cot and put a hand on his.

"No, Buck, the hunt. I meant what happened after we left?"

"What do you think happened? I killed them."

"I just—"

"I'd rather not talk about it."

"Okay, I'll leave you alone. But I'll be back when the doctor gets here."

What was it with women? Always wanted to *discuss* everything. He had another slug of gin. What had happened in the bush that morning was probably the best shooting of his career, and although he didn't feel like discussing it, he did wish somebody had been there to see how cleanly he dispatched the five beasts. Well, four of them were clean anyway. The leopard had circled around in the grass and lunged for him. Fortunately Buck had studied judo for precisely such a situation and was able to put an *Ura-nage* (rear throw) on it, but not before it raked the living hell out of his shoulder, taking damn chunks out of him. It was all Buck could do to draw his pistol and pump that cat full of lead. By the time Murubi and the crew returned, he was wearing a dead leopard as a blanket.

The damn buff had taken three shots to kill, and the rhino had worried him for a moment, too, what with it skidding to a stop three feet short of Buck's chest. The elephant, surprisingly, went down with one shot. Shoot, pivot, shoot—each time the heavy gun's report splitting the air. With his last rifle shell, he hit the lion as it charged, and shut the animal down. He was catching his breath when he realized he'd forgotten about the leopard. Which is how he got here, on the cot with a torn-up shoulder, drinking Plymouth Navy Strength.

That he hadn't been killed was not a relief; it was distressing. He knew he was going to die on this safari, but if a gang of Africa's deadliest beasts wasn't able to kill him, what was his fate? He'd always lived an existential life, being present in every moment—a kind of concentration he'd learned from the Masai, whose entire culture was centered around hunting. Not over-thinking things had been a lifelong habit, and suddenly he was seized by deep questions about how his life would end. It was rubbish.

He fell asleep with the bottle still clutched in his fingers and was awakened by Nora with the doctor. They stitched him up and sedated him, and the next time he awoke it was daylight. Someone was screaming.

"God, it hurts!"

Buck eased off the cot and went outside. It was that idiot husband. He'd convinced Harris to take him out that morning and let him try one of the big doubles with Nitro Express cartridges. Holding it wrong and firing both barrels simultaneously, the fool had broken his damn clavicle.

"He'll have to go to hospital," Buck said.

"He won't go to African hospitals," Nora said.

"Then he'll have to go home. We can't set that kind of bone in camp. What did the doctor say?"

"Exactly that."

"So this is goodbye then."

"For them it is." She nodded at the Rover, where the Nathansons were helping her weeping husband get in. "But I'm not giving up a safari just because he doesn't know how to shoot a gun. I'll see them to the plane, then be back to take care of you."

"Don't trouble yourself," he said.

"It's no trouble. You need nursing."

Buck said goodbye and returned to his tent. He spent the rest of the morning into the afternoon staring through the mosquito netting at a distant green hill shrouded in mist. As the day wore on, he started looking for the Rover to return. There and back, Buck estimated, would take six hours, eight tops. He sipped gin, smoked Chesterfields, read Yeats. By dusk he had turned on his side to better see her when she returned and shook out that blonde hair of hers. As Yeats writes, "Only God, my dear/Could love you for yourself alone/And not your yellow hair."

Now in his mind he saw a redhead—Miss Penelope Wainwright, the British banker's daughter—and he remembered how good she made a pair of jodhpurs look. It was 1942, he was a responsible 17 to her spoiled 22, and in case no one got the memo, there was a war on. Certain she'd be safe in the wilds of Africa, her father had sent her on safari after the Blitz, unaware that the damn Nazis were here, too, as they were everywhere, like cockroaches. The soldiers stationed here were deformed or damaged in some way, some missing limbs, others with brutal shell-shock that left them twitching at their dusty posts. Still, they hunted Brits, and Buck was made her gun-bearer and bodyguard.

They were tracking a lion, an ancient male that somehow had retained control of his pride, into deep scrubby brush. It was only a week before the rains came and the far horizon had its steel-blue glow and the winds had begun to shift. The party had split up, and, following orders, Buck stayed three feet from Penelope at all times, close enough that he could always smell her. Unlike other women, her scent wasn't brash perfume but rather when he found himself downwind of her, especially if he happened by the nape of her neck in close quarters, the word that came to mind was *fresh*. Hiking back to camp, talking and laughing, they parted some branches and saw a German troop transport with its wheels stuck and its soldiers halfheartedly pushing with cigarettes hanging from their lips. One of them spotted her red hair and shouted to the others. Buck noticed four of them lined up front to back, trained the .600 on the first one's neck, and dropped all four with a single shot. He grabbed Penelope by the wrist and hauled her into the brush. For two days they knew how it felt to be hunted like the lions he had so casually pursued, but in the end, the German platoon, rendered a dozen men smaller by Buck, gave up the chase.

Safe finally they made camp and she proved herself a highly sportive girl, and when the rains came and he ceased to work for her, it was even better. Afternoons in the hotel room with the rain streaming off the roof like Victoria Falls, safely entwined in the cool sheets, ample gin and cigarettes within arm's reach, the two of them made love all day long, then dined in a corner of the hotel restaurant beside the open window that looked out at the nonstop rain where it dripped from the eaves over the veranda. On that veranda she read aloud to him from months-old newspapers about the war, sitting on his lap in the wide rocking chair, until the chirping lilt of her voice and the rhythm of the chair stirred his groin and she was almost noticeably elevated, like a lorry by a jack, and she looked at him with a surprise and amusement that never diminished and, dropping the paper, led him back to the room.

In the evenings by lamplight she spoke of home, of her family's townhouse overlooking Hyde Park, of their summer home in Marseilles which her father knew the Nazis were occupying, and of how much she wanted him to visit one day. *Visit?* After he had already held her in his arms for more hours than couples married a lifetime, all she wanted him to do was visit? For the months they had cohabited, she said she loved him. They had slain lions and leopards and Germans together. He had protected her at every turn.

And then the telegram came. Its contents she never shared, but in the morning when she was gone and only the scent of her remained, he knew she had abandoned him for England, and that she had been ordered to by her family. Yet he went to the railway station to look for her, and the platform, usually an obstacle course of natives and travelers arriving in hope or leaving in shame, was starkly empty save a lone porter pushing a hand-truck of whiskey. When Buck asked about a red-haired woman the porter showed his enviable teeth and pointed at the smoke-stained horizon. At that moment he became Buck Remington, Great White Hunter, vowing never again to let himself feel, and never again to believe a word a woman said.

Which is why, in the cool of the gathering evening as he lay on the cot, Buck found it so curious that he was gazing across the plain for the faintest flicker of head-lights, as though Nora had told him the truth when she said she'd return. For a few hours he had allowed himself to imagine her leaving that rich pansy and himself retiring from the hunt, maybe writing a book. His hopes were highest at midday, but as the sun set, his dreams died with the light.

When the Rover finally whirred back into camp and only one door open and shut, Buck knew. Murubi entered the tent and solemnly handed him a note:

Buck,
It would have been wonderful, I'm sure, but I can't jeopardize the life I have with Kendall. Besides, the great Buck Remington doesn't need me. Tomorrow some other woman will be in your cot and you will have forgotten all about little Nora Cameron. I hope to see you again someday, perhaps in the States.
Take care of yourself.
Love,
Nora

He lit another Chesterfield, burned the note and tossed the cinder on the wooden tent floor. Another few belts of gin, and when he lay down again the pain reached in from the wound on his shoulder and squeezed his chest. He went on smoking, ignoring the crushing sensation in his chest, not bothering to call out to anyone. This, he supposed, was how his wounded prey had felt when hiding in thick cover.

Closing his eyes, Buck Remington gave a final snorting smile at Death. After decades in the bush, this was how the old bastard would finally get him. As he drifted off, his being was filled with the cheer of campfire singing, the tang of roasting meat, and the night sounds of Africa.

THE MAGNIFICENT MURPHY

In my younger and more vulnerable years my literature professor gave me some advice that I've been turning over in my mind ever since.

"Whenever you feel like reading unauthorized sequels or derivatives of literary classics," he said, "just remember that such fiction is garbage and its authors deserve to die."

He didn't say any more on the subject, but as a man who had bolted across academic No Man's Land from the philosophy of language to American literature, he was inclined to be uncomfortably direct in his first expression of an idea. In consequence, I haven't forgotten any of his epigrams, and I fear his brand of literary wisdom has been so deeply etched in my consciousness that like the hieroglyphics left in praise of long-departed Pharaohs, his uncompromising views will stay with me forever.

For three generations my family have been prominent, well-to-do Midwesterners, and as such tacitly disapproved of my wasting my potential (and my father's money) on the literary arts. Therefore in the spring of 1922 I moved to New York and plunged into the bond business.

The wanton depravity with which I spent that spring and summer, in the company of Tom and cousin Daisy, Jordan and Gatsby, I have already documented elsewhere.

However, if a piece of literature is defined as much by its omissions as by its contents, then perhaps it is a blessing to readers that I left out certain incidents in my first account, such as my botched attempt at polo with Tom, and my introduction to Gatsby's other next-door neighbor—the only person besides Gatsby who represented everything for which I have an unaffected scorn—author Martin Michaels-Murphy.

Early in my residence at the mean little bungalow that quaked in the shadow of Gatsby's mansion like a tick beneath a Burmese elephant, I stumbled into the kitchen one rainy Saturday to find my Finnish housekeeper jabbing at bacon while reading a book. The bacon strips suffered horribly from her divided loyalties, smoldering like Inquisition victims in a fire pit.

I couldn't imagine what book could captivate her so, particularly since she was unable to read or speak English, a fact that had caused more than a few awkward silences between us. I tilted the book cover toward the window. An etching showed a sperm whale swimming topside, smoking a pipe and wearing a deerstalker cap. The text was all in Finnish, save the author's name, a name with which I was not yet familiar: Martin Michaels-Murphy.

I confess that I forgot about the book entirely until one clear evening before Gatsby's latest rollicking affair when I was strolling across his blue lawn and spied the manor lord holding his nightly vigil. Hands in his pockets, he stared across the lapping water at the green light on Daisy's shore. Mingled with the din of the tuning orchestra, the ballistic chatter of a typewriter trickled down the long hill to Gatsby and me. My host glanced at a pocket watch, lingering obviously so that I would see the thick gold chain and emerald fob with his initials spelled out in small diamonds. He turned to me with one of his perfectly rehearsed smiles.

"Good evening, old sport."

"My, that's quite a watch fob," I said.

"Oh, this? Just a little something I had a Swiss jeweler put together for me." He held it up to the waning sunset. "The diamonds are real. So's the emerald. Four karats."

"Remarkable."

"Would you like one, old sport?" he asked.

"No thanks."

The weary sighs of tuning instruments faded, and in their place rose up the chortling of distant motor boats skimming the courtesy bay, and the unnatural clacking of that typewriter. I wondered if this was the pestilent noise that had caused me to wake inexplicably from my slumbers at one o'clock every morning.

"Don't tell me they're adding a typewriter to the orchestra," I said.

Gatsby had been gazing at the green light as though he were a plant that drew life from it. He closed his eyes and bowed his head, and when he turned to me again he stood with the surety of a sequoia.

"Typewriter? Yes, that's Murphy. Writer, lives next door."

"A writer? Not *Martin* Murphy by any chance."

"Sure. I've got all his books. Come up to the house, old sport, I'll show you."

In his library, gold leaf from myriad book spines glared so fiercely from the wall that I was forced to squint. Gatsby posed beside a shelf with a fist on his hip and glided his free hand across them. A few titles caught my attention:

Crime and Punishment and Mutant Cossacks
Hamlet the Ghoul Dane
Moby Dick, Sea Detective
Sense & Sensibility—with Gypsy Mayhem!

"Have you read them?" I asked.

"Not yet. Haven't found the time."

I reached for the Moby Dick volume. The pages, like those of all of my host's books, were uncut; however, I gleaned enough from one passage to grasp the whole, and quickly reshelved it.

"Would you like to meet him?" Gatsby asked. "He's a pleasant enough chap."

"Doesn't he come to your parties?"

Gatsby sighed. "No, unfortunately. He writes at night."

His deflated posture said he considered it an unforgivable flaw in his own character that he hadn't been able to entice the elusive Mr. Murphy to his vespertine riots. Gradually his face illuminated like a full moon emerging from a cloud over the sleeping Sound.

"But I'll tell you what, old sport. Tomorrow afternoon, we'll pay him a visit."

———◆◆◆———

An English box hedge two fathoms high separated Gatsby's forty acres from Mr. Murphy's six, and at precisely three o'clock the next afternoon Gatsby led me through an archway built into the greenery and across a stretch of grass that was the poor and sickly nephew of his own rich lawn. The twang of a tennis racquet floated on the muggy silence. A pair of familiar-looking windows sneered at me from atop a knoll. The house was an exact model, perhaps one-third scale, of Gatsby's replica of the Hôtel de Ville in Normandy.

Gatsby laughed. "Hah, it got you, too. Murphy's idea. Thought it'd be amusing."

"Imitation is the highest form of flattery, they say."

"Quite true, quite true."

By way of a fence gate we entered a capacious courtyard of sanguine clay, in the center of which was a tennis court. A bearded and bespectacled young man, not five years older than I, glided back and forth on the baseline as hypnotically as a birch in an autumn breeze, the sparkling white of his tennis costume heightening the effect. Across the net a balding man in butler's dress removed balls from a wicker trough. With a stiff arm, he tossed one at a time at the man in white, who with grace and flourish proceeded to hit each ball far over the opposite fence.

"Not so fast, Johnson," said the man in white. "Oh, Gatsby!"

"Hello, old sport."

I must admit to feeling a trifle jealous when Gatsby referred to him by a moniker that I thought was reserved solely for me.

"Murph, I'd like you to meet my neighbor, Nick Carraway. Nick, Martin Murphy."

We shook hands. His was clammy and had all the rigidity of wet bread.

"Actually, Gatsby," he said, "it's Michaels-Murphy."

"Sorry, old sport, I keep forgetting."

"Is Michaels your middle name?" I asked.

"No, it's my mother's family's surname. The two are hyphenated."

"I've never heard of such a thing."

It struck me as indecisive and pretentious, worse than Gatsby's gauche habit of monogramming everything he owned, but as one inclined to reserve all judgments, I said nothing further on the matter.

"It's becoming rather popular in my circles," he said. "It won't be long before *all* men are hyphenating their last names." He bounced his racquet on his knee, as though gaveling the debate to a close. "So, Gatsby, what brings you by?"

"Nick here was interested in your books."

"Well, actually—"

Gatsby's butler appeared at the gate.

"Pittsburgh on the line, sir."

"You'll have to excuse me. Have fun, old sports."

He left with the butler. When I turned around, Mr. Michaels-Murphy was at a table beneath an umbrella, sipping a pink libation.

"Lemonade, Nick. With something extra. Care to wet your whistle?"

"Why not?" I sat down, noticing that the sun's surly glare was in my eyes but not Murphy's. He poured a glass and slid it across the table.

"So, Nick. Which of my books have you read?"

"No, it was my housekeeper. She was reading your Moby Dick story—in Finnish." I looked around. "You must be very successful."

"Well, my books *have* been published in multiple languages, and I *do* have this place." He waved his hand like the first half of a magic spell.

"I notice your books use other writers' characters," I said. "Have you ever written anything entirely your own?"

"What do you mean 'entirely my own'? They might not be my characters as you say, but I give them new adventures and use alternate points of view. A lot of people love my work, you know." He topped off our glasses. "Say, would you like to stay for dinner? Gatsby had some lobsters flown down from Maine this morning, and my guests can't make it. It would be a travesty to waste them."

At the corners of his eyes and mouth I detected flickers of desperation in his otherwise stoic face. Like Gatsby, he was a man with time and toys, but no one to play with. Pity bubbled up in me. However, I was expected elsewhere that evening.

"I'm sorry, but I have another engagement—my cousin, Daisy." I pointed toward East Egg. "Perhaps you've heard of her?"

"Afraid I don't get over there much. Another time then."

He stood and I followed him up curving marble stairs to a croquet green. In the center stood a voluminous white gazebo with a crimson pennant flag flapping jadedly on the peak. Shoulders back, chin erect, Murphy tossed his tennis racquet on the grass and walked into the tent's ample shade with the confidence of a Hindu maharajah.

"Nick, old sport," he said, "*this* is where the magic happens."

Not wanting his calling me "old sport" to become precedent, I refused to respond.

It was precisely the sort of workspace someone who romanticized writing would contrive: a broad mahogany table facing the ocean, a stack of crisp bond held in place by a stone, and an Underwood typewriter slightly smaller than an airplane engine. Murphy rolled in a sheet and typed a message to me:

I HAVE A SIGNING AT SCRIBNER'S SATUR-DAY NEXT. WOULD YOU CARE TO JOIN ME?

I didn't, but I intuited from his having typed the question that he feared I would say no.

"Certainly," I said.

GREAT!

His butler entered the tent. "That hate mail you requested, sir."

"Same handwriting, Johnson?"

"I believe so, sir."

Murphy snatched the letter, scanned it and thrust it at me. Immediately I recognized the author as my literature professor at New Haven. His scrawl was inimitable: *"Mr. Murphy, cease writing these insulting imitations or there will be <u>violent</u> consequences. — The Literati."*

"Needless to say," Murphy said, "I get quite a bit of the stuff. But this gentleman, the spokesman for this so-called *Literati,* whoever he is, takes the cake. He's been sending me death threats for years." He handed the letter back to Johnson. "Put it with the others."

Murphy cranked down the page.

GOOD TO MEET YOU, NICK. UNTIL NEXT SATURDAY. NOW IF YOU'LL EXCUSE ME, I HAVE

LOBSTERS TO EAT AND PAGES TO TYPE. JOHNSON WILL DRIVE YOU HOME.

"That's okay," I said, "I can walk."

As I stepped away, I heard Murphy muttering to himself: "O Divine Poesy, goddess, daughter of Zeus, sustain for me this tale of the various minded man..." I asked Johnson about it.

"The Invocation of the Muse, sir. From *The Odyssey.* Mr. Michaels-Murphy begins every writing session with it."

"I see. Thank you, Johnson."

At the office the following week, as if testy from the sizzling days and sweltering nights, the sales manager, a barrel-chested doppelgänger of Colonel Roosevelt, swiftly patrolled the sales floor with his hands clasped behind his back. His demeanor made for many nervous moments since all of my acquaintances had chosen that week to telephone me relentlessly.

"So, old sport," Gatsby said, "when are we taking my hydroplane out? And don't forget my swimming pool. We haven't used it all summer."

"Darling Nick," Daisy chirped, "I'm so *dreadfully* bored. Tell me, does New York miss me?"

"Now listen to this, Nick," Tom said. "I've got Goddard's book right here. The Mexes, Nick. The Mexes are going to take it all! We've got to do something!"

The only phone call I took with alacrity was from a classmate of mine at New Haven, Elton White, who was a now a struggling writer living downtown. He'd had a couple of short stories published in the little magazines, but lacked connections to advance further. My upcoming engagement with Murphy came to mind. Detecting despair in my old friend's voice, I said that I was coming into town on the week-end with a best-selling writer and that I would ask him to drop by.

"Oh, that would be great of you, Nick! And please tell Mr. Murphy how much I appreciate this."

When Murphy called, I relayed my plan and Elton's message.

"That's fine," Murphy said. "Glad to help a fellow writer out."

However, as we drove through the Valley of Ashes that Saturday morning, Murphy's benevolence appeared to have evaporated.

"Nick, so who is this Elton White?"

"I told you, an old friend."

"I don't know what he expects from me."

"He doesn't *expect* anything," I said curtly. "I hoped if you liked his work, you might pass it along to your publisher."

He produced an unlit pipe and clenched it in his teeth. His woolen touring cap was pulled low on his forehead, forcing him to tilt his head back to see through the narrow windshield.

"Maybe. If his writing's any good, that is."

To fortify his automobile for the second half of our journey, we stopped at Wilson's service station in the unwavering gaze of Dr. T.J. Eckleburg. I suddenly remembered that I had agreed to lunch at Daisy's, and as I went inside the station to telephone my regrets, I glimpsed Myrtle Wilson, a haggard Rapunzel, in the tiny window above the garage bay.

The moment I entered that dank coolness redolent of fumes and failure, Wilson alighted from a stool and placed a book he had been reading face-down. I relayed my message to Daisy's butler, and on my way out glanced at the book cover: *Moby Dick, Sea Detective*. Wilson and I shared a nod as we passed each other. Once on the motor-road again, I asked Murphy whether he knew that Wilson was a fan.

"No, I didn't," he said. "Then again, I have *many* fans."

By a series of serpentine maneuvers we arrived at Elton White's building on the Lower East Side. His landlady, a plump virago, intercepted us at the door and waved dismissively up a set of stairs that leaned more precipitously from the wall the higher we went. Finally reaching Elton's door, I knocked briskly, relieved to put the perilous and exhausting climb behind us.

Pallid and round-shouldered, Elton was hardly the ruddy and robust friend I remembered from college. His once luminous blonde hair had grayed and gone defiantly crooked. He smiled and shook my hand as if he hadn't had a visitor in months.

"Nick! Please, come in, come in!"

For some reason I had expected to walk into a room with piles of malodorous laundry and the tinge of ammonia; however, we were instead treated to the spartan inside of Thoreau's cabin. The most extravagant feature—a large window with a view of the Brooklyn Bridge—served only to accentuate the austerity of the tiny space: bed, dresser, table, chair.

Murphy assumed a quietly horrified countenance, as though the surroundings were too vivid a reminder of a past he wished to forget. He commandeered the chair and sat with his arms draped over the back.

"Mr. Murphy," Elton said, "thank you so much for coming."

"It's *Michaels*-Murphy," he said, squeezing Elton's fingers in a half-handshake, "but sure, no problem." He consulted a pocket watch and took out his unlit pipe. "We should probably get to it."

"Yes, right." Elton grabbed two sheaves of papers, and with minutely trembling hands gave us each one. "Mr. Michaels-Murphy, do you need a match?"

"No, no, just let me read."

"I'm going for a walk," Elton said.

I sat on the bed and began. Five sentences in, I knew where the luminosity of Elton's hair had gone: into his writing. The first story was about a young woman who through subterfuge and luck becomes a flying ace in the Great War, shooting down a dozen Germans before getting shot down herself and raped by her own men. It left me breathless and hollow. For his second story, he drew on his summers as a teenage boy in Maine. A father hires a local young man—a native islander—to "toughen the boy up," an arrangement that inexorably leads to the boy attempting to swim between islands in a storm and drowning. I wiped my eyes.

"Please, you're *crying*?" Murphy glanced at the door. "Don't misunderstand me, he's got potential, but depressing work like this will never sell."

"Couldn't you at least show them to your editor?"

"Look, Nick," he said, pointing at me with the pipe, "I'm a *writer*. You're a sensitive fellow, and so is this friend of yours, and maybe the two of you could be writers, but I *am* a writer, understand?"

"Not really," I said. "I always thought a writer was one who writes."

"Hah! That's what amateurs think. A writer is one who sells, Nick. *Sells!*"

I waved my sheaf at him. "But maybe these could sell. Why not show them to your editor?"

"I'll be down in the car." He tossed his copies on the bed and left.

I folded mine and put them in my pocket. The room was suddenly twice as small and I wished I worked in publishing. On my way out, I knocked over a stack of library books, sending a typewriter pawn slip across the floor. I took a sawbuck out of my wallet and put it on the table with the pawn slip. Elton met me halfway down the stairs. He clutched the dismal bannister as if debating throwing himself over the edge.

"He didn't like them, did he?"

"They're not his cup of tea, but I think they're excellent." I tapped my jacket. "I'm giving them to his editor."

"Oh, what's the use?" Elton said. "He's the writer."

"Believe me, you're better." A horn blared on the street. "I'll call as soon as I hear anything."

Murphy's book launch for his *Vanity Fair* knockoff—*Becky Sharp, Werewolf*—had all of the glittering earmarks of a Jay Gatsby production. Therefore, I wasn't at all surprised when I learned that Gatsby had paid for the entire thing—including, it seemed, the fine weather. Beneath a sparkling cerulean firmament, a line of several hundred fans stretched from Scribner's quivering doors three blocks down Fifth Avenue. A jazz band scorched the air from a parked parade float. A chorus line of women in gold crepe flapper dresses performed the Charleston with mechanical precision. And for the *pièce de résistance*, a barnstormer buzzed straight down Fifth Avenue, scant yards from the pavement, with an interminable banner snaking behind the plane: "*BECKY SHARP, WERE-WOLF* BY MARTIN MICHAELS-MURPHY — BUY IT TODAY!"

Murphy's editor, a young man whose facial hair had yet to make its mark on the world, watched with his face waging a private war between panic and rapture, the latter eventually triumphant. When the biplane finished its second pass, before the fog of adrenaline had lifted I introduced myself as a friend of Gatsby's and handed him Elton's stories.

"Oh, Gatsby! You know him?"

"I do. I'm his neighbor."

"I'm going to his party tonight. I hear his parties are quite wonderful."

"Yes, wonderful. So, my friend's stories—you'll read them?"

"For Gatsby? Of course!"

<hr />

The after-effects of Gatsby's party celebrating "Murph's" book launch still clung to me Monday evening when I trudged up my bungalow steps and paused to unlock the kitchen door. At the end of the porch, silhouetted by the gloaming, a man sat in the porch swing with his hands in his lap.

"May I help you?" I asked.

"Hello, Nicholas."

I couldn't place his voice, and in the end it was his monkish posture that triggered my memory.

"Professor? What brings you here?"

"I understand you are friends with the infamous Mr. Murphy."

I sat in a chair beside the swing. The thought lines in the Professor's forehead were more deeply rutted, but otherwise—tall, lean, full head of hair—he seemed not to have aged a day since New Haven.

"I'd hardly call us friends," I said. "He's a neighbor, that's all. But clearly *you* know him. I saw your latest death threat."

"Nicholas," he said, rocking gently, "have you ever wondered, if we could talk to Miss Austen or Mr. Melville, how they would feel about their literary creations being bastardized? There is a legacy of literature, my boy, and the organization of which I am a part—the Literati—has a centuries-old mandate of protecting that legacy. By the way, *this* was on the door when I got here."

He handed me a typewritten note from Murphy, inviting me fishing on the weekend.

"Should you decide to go with him," he continued, "there's something you should know. The man can't swim."

"Excuse me, sir," I said, pocketing the note, "Murphy is a selfish, pandering, no-talent fop, but I'm certainly not going to do what you're suggesting."

The Professor picked up his hat, walked to the porch steps and paused. He thumped the hat against his leg.

"I'm afraid I have some bad news," he said. "Elton White jumped off the Brooklyn Bridge this morning. It seems Mr. Murphy found out you had spoken to his editor, and he made him telephone Elton and tell him his writing was abysmal and that he could never be a writer. It was more than Elton could take. I'm sorry."

Vaguely I heard the screen door creak and slap shut, and for what seemed like hours I was paralyzed in that chair, barely able to breathe. Finally I stumbled inside and telephoned the police to confirm the Professor's report. It was true. And as a final indignity to poor Elton, his landlady had identified the body.

——◆·◆·◆——

Of Elton, his death, and his Connecticut funeral my memory was green when I stepped aboard Murphy's cabin cruiser in the silvery half-light. I cast off the lines while Murphy eased the boat away from the dock. We furrowed the flat waters. Pockets of wispy fog swirled away at our craft's approach. The air was sultry enough to swim in, and as it buffed my cheek I stared at Murphy's dark back where he stood at the helm. He wasn't wearing a life vest. I recalled the Professor's words: *"The man can't swim."*

Some miles out, Murphy stopped the boat and stood facing the dawn with the same tremulousness as Gatsby venerating Daisy's green light. Sunrise at sea, and a glass sea at that, is at once a wondrous and mesmerizing experience, for the instant the sun appears on your side of the world the water is set aflame, with every conceivable hue dancing before your eyes. If ever there were a perfect moment to dispose of something at sea, this was it.

"Why did you do it, Martin?"

"Pardon?"

"Tell your editor to criticize Elton. He took his own life because of it, you know."

Murphy continued to face the sunrise.

"Did he? Well, probably for the best then. Writing is an extremely competitive field and an unforgiving mistress. It takes a stony heart. If Elton wasn't strong enough, it's better that he went now, rather than forty years from now, bitter and disillusioned."

"Excuse me?"

Murphy spun around, and whether made dizzy by the violence of his motion or whether momentarily blinded from the sun, the effect was the same: he stumbled backward, catching the backs of his legs against the side of the boat, and fell overboard.

As I sat there listening to his watery yelps and frantic scratches at the hull, I wondered if this was Fate intervening, performing the action of which I was clearly incapable. But this wouldn't do. I was from a family of God-fearing, well-to-do Midwesterners—people who simply did not let a man drown, even if he deserved such an end.

I sprang from my seat and grabbed him by the collar.

Once he had hauled himself out by the ladder and emerged from below-decks where he had changed clothes, Murphy opened his mouth to say something, but I held up a hand. I feared that if his comment was in any way unapologetic or snide, I might shove him overboard and leave him this time.

The aptness and irony with which the universe sometimes metes out punishment is enough to make a man tremble, as though he stands not in the cold unwavering gaze of Dr. T.J. Eckleburg, but of the Creator Himself. I realized how puny my attempt at avenging Elton's death would have been once I saw the fearsome way so many disparate people and events coalesced to bring about Murphy's end.

For the rest of that summer I had no contact with Mr. Michaels-Murphy and instead re-boarded the private railroad car of Gatsby, Daisy and Tom, unaware that Fate was at the controls of the locomotive and that the brakeless train was plummeting towards disaster. The upshot—Myrtle's death by Daisy's poor driving, Gatsby's assuming the blame, Tom's informing Wilson of Gatsby's whereabouts, Wilson's shooting of Gatsby and taking his own life—is well documented in my first account. Previously unknown, however, is how the carelessness and solipsism of that cursed quintet conspired to destroy Murphy as well.

The day after Gatsby's staff and I discovered the master of the house floating dead in his pool, and his murderer in the grass with a bullet through his head, Johnson came shakily from next door and informed me that *his* master had been killed as well. Recreating the timeline, detectives determined that Wilson had first shot Murphy, realized he'd made a mistake, and then shot Gatsby. And rather than killing himself solely over the death of his wife, as the authorities first thought, Wilson, they conjectured, had been so overcome with guilt and remorse for shooting the author of the only book he'd ever read, that he planted his pistol against his own temple and fired. Weeks later, while raking leaves, Murphy's gardener found Wilson's copy of *Moby Dick, Sea Detective*, its pages foxed and yellowed from rain and sun.

As devoutly as Gatsby believed in the green light, Murphy believed in the divine Poesy, and in her eventual willingness to electrify his imagination and help him to create a work of literary genius—an ambition far beyond the pale cast of his thought. But it was not to be. Forever relegated to peering into the club of fine literature from a street window, Murphy had had to content himself with infinite international sales, a miniature mansion by the sea, and adoration from semi-literate fans.

And so he typed on, convinced that tomorrow or the next day Poesy would bless him, when in fact with each page, with each new book, he was actually digging—digging his own hole of obscurity deeper and deeper.

—For F. Scott Fitzgerald

Sonata for Knife & Violin in D ♭ Major; Op. 1 "Revenge"

I. *Allegro; vita dalla morte*

At the moment he plunged the chef's knife into Vito's chest and heard the crack of the bastard's breastplate, Nikolai Vernikov recalled the similar sound of a watermelon breaking open. That afternoon he had eaten an entire melon himself, hacking off chunks and devouring them over the sink. He ate, practiced, and ate again. It was the first time he'd ever eaten with abandon, having always sat at a dining table for meals or snacks of any size. Slapping the blade into the pink pulp, feeling the sticky water drip down his hands and chin, he sensed a switch go on in his brain, awakening an unfamiliar, primordial side of himself and sparking a long-smoldering desire to kill Vito.

Between his career as a concert violinist and his hobby of building model ships in bottles, Nikolai's entire life had been a study in precision. He had never swung a baseball bat or even thrown a punch. Since the violin was his livelihood, to prevent injury to his hands he wore black leather gloves everywhere he went, even in summer, and he wore them now as he thrust the knife deeper into Vito.

Vito's nostrils flared. He clawed at Nikolai's shoulders. As Vito sank to the floor, he tried to speak but the gurgling of blood muffled his voice. Whatever the idiot had tried to say, Nikolai knew it wasn't an apology.

Standing over the body, basking in the astonishment frozen on Vito's face, Nikolai drifted away to the summer of '77, when his family escaped from the Ukraine to Brooklyn. Almost immediately, and for no conceivable reason but to be cruel, Vito and his friends began to torment him and his sister Katerina, calling them "Commie bastards," punching him, lifting Katerina's skirt, spreading rumors through school that Nikolai's father was a Soviet spy. He and his sister pleaded with their parents to move, but they refused and the situation worsened, culminating in Vito and his gang ambushing Nikolai, hurling baseballs at his head, and smashing his violin—a gift from his grandfather in Minsk. Bruised and sobbing, he ran home, took his father's rifle from the closet, and sat on the bed weighing his two options: either kill them or kill himself. Luckily his mother found him before he could choose, and they finally moved away.

Nikolai yanked the knife out of Vito's lifeless body, carried it to the kitchen and washed it off in the sink. Some blood had sprayed on his face and gloves; that got washed off, too. He wiped the 12-inch chef's knife dry and returned it to his gym bag. As for the poncho covering his clothes, he would dispose of it elsewhere.

Tomorrow morning was his audition for first violin—*concertmaster*—with his orchestra, the New York Symphony, and he wanted to get in an hour's practice before bed. Conductors, critics, and his fellow musicians concurred: Nikolai was a superlative technician—a human metronome with freakishly perfect pitch; however, they also agreed that his play was an emotional desert, which was why he could never expect higher placement in the orchestra. A small, *pianissimo* voice inside him was determined to prove them wrong.

II. *Presto; essere giocato come se in un trance*

Maestro Holbrook Robinson squinted over his reading glasses as Nikolai strode onto the stage.

"Mister Vernikov? I didn't know you were auditioning."

"It is an open call, is it not?"

"Yes, but…"

Nikolai held the violin to his ear and plucked the strings. The violin was ready, and so was he. The Maestro sighed and leaned back in his chair.

"Very well, but we need to stay on shedshule, so if you please." He waved for Nikolai to get on with it.

Nikolai handed the score to the bald-headed pianist, who frowned as soon as he read it.

"The *Kreutzer?* Overkill, don't you think?"

"Not for first violin." Nikolai stared at the pianist.

"I'm not sure if—"

"Just follow my lead." Nikolai lifted violin and bow simultaneously. "Open adagio and build to presto."

Of Beethoven's sonatas for violin and piano, Sonata No. 9 in A major—the Kreutzer—and especially its tempestuous first movement, which Nikolai was about to play—demonstrated virtuosity with the violin more than any other. Months earlier when he learned that the then-concertmaster, Eric Chen, was leaving for the

London Philharmonic, Nikolai had decided to use this piece to showcase his skills. He knew the Maestro believed he lacked the charisma necessary to captivate an audience, but ever since he'd joined the Orchestra he had coveted First Chair. Now with a chance to seize it, Nikolai was prepared to bare his soul and suffer the Maestro's venomous critique afterwards.

The plaintive opening strains of the Kreutzer failed to get the Maestro's attention; Robinson chatted with one of the board members instead of watching Nikolai. However, as the tempo accelerated, Nikolai forgot all about the audition and gave himself wholly to the music. He loved this piece, with its harmonic interplay, its musical cat and mouse between piano and violin. His accompanist was ideal, maintaining even time and keeping grandiose flourishes to a minimum. And with the piano subdued, Nikolai's strings soared to sublime heights. Usually while playing, Nikolai had a mental image of his body as a musical machine, his bow arm a great driving piston and his fingers flying up and down the fingerboard, compressing and releasing strings like so many valves opening and closing shut. Now, though, with the music coursing through him he gave no thought to mechanics. His torso swayed in time, although he wasn't directly aware of that either. It was as though he were hovering over his body, and for the first time in 32 years of playing he ceased to see the notes in his head—trailing past his mind's eye like a stock ticker—and instead perceived the music the way Beethoven had intended it—as a transfer of pure emotion. A hot flush washed down his neck, through his arms, into the instrument. Suddenly he understood the composer's tortured mind when creating this piece: his soaring, joyous highs, and his abysmal, homicidal lows.

Sweat trickled down his temples, which was unusual because he never perspired during a performance. What was wrong? His fingers buzzed, his bow arm throbbed. Plucking his way through the pizzicato sequence, glimpses of Vito's murder came to him—thrusting the knife in, gritting his teeth in ecstasy of the bloodlust, reveling in what had to be Vito's final realization: that Nikolai had gotten his revenge. The relief was rapturous; it reminded him of his father's tears of joy when they arrived in America. Killing his former tormentor had given him life, and that life now resounded through his violin.

In the remaining bars of the piece, Nikolai lost awareness of the notes entirely. He felt himself atop a magnificent stallion in a driving gallop for the finish. Always he had held back; but this time, into these final few notes, he put the last full measure of his devotion: his years of practice, his hopes, his fears—his very *life* he gave to this music, resolved that if God should strike him down there and then, he would die a contented man.

He scraped the bow across the strings for the last note and dropped his arms in exhaustion. When he opened his eyes, the Maestro was on his feet, clapping.

"Nikolai Vernikov!" The Maestro came to him, cupped Nikolai's face in his hands. "Where did this come from?"

The murder. There was no other explanation. Nikolai pulled out a handkerchief and patted his brow.

"Steady practice," he said. "Practice, and channeling my emotions, I suppose."

III. *Adagio espressivo; azione aumentante, complicazioni*

Between July and November—a four-month period of waiting for the Symphony to begin its new season— Nikolai played in the Moonlight String Quartet. Whether a city-sponsored concert, a fundraising gala at the Waldorf-Astoria, or a private party, the Quartet took whatever work it could get to pay the bills and stay sharp for the next season. This Sunday they had just finished a fiftieth wedding anniversary party at a Fifth Avenue penthouse overlooking Central Park. The October foliage sparkled in the late afternoon sun, and although it was cool, he decided to walk through the park to his West Side apartment.

Outside, he crossed Fifth Avenue and cut into the park at 81ˢᵗ Street, next to the Met. He was a hundred feet in, strolling past a touch football game, when behind him the *presto* clip-clop of a woman's shoes and the grinding sound of rolling wheels echoed on the asphalt path.

"Nikolai, wait!"

It was Jane Halstead, cellist in the Symphony and the Quartet. She ran unsteadily toward him, hauling the cello case behind her. Nikolai froze. He had no idea what to say. The black party dress hugged her petite body and stood out sharply against the fiery red of a sugar maple behind her. He longed to scoop her in his arms, carry her to a pile of freshly fallen leaves, and feel her fragility beneath him.

She caught up and put a hand to her chest. Her breath was ragged. During rehearsal breaks, Jane routinely smoked outside the Symphony stage door until the last minute.

"Hey, I've been…meaning to tell you. Congrats on first chair."

"Thank you."

Recently Nikolai's sense of smell had become strangely acute. Although he had been close to Jane countless times before, this was the first time he detected a fragrance around her. But it wasn't perfume or soapy skin; the piquant scent was faint as a whisper, yet it gave his nose the same prickly sensation as ozone after a thunderstorm. With a smile he realized it was her lusty pheromones he smelled. She nudged him with her shoulder.

"*So*…who'd you have to kill?"

His eyes shot open. "*What?*"

"C'mon, Maestro's a sonovabitch," she said. "I thought for sure he'd go with someone from outside. What'd you do, bump off some Cleveland hack?"

"No, just practice."

"Sure, that's what they all say." Jane rubbed her chest with her free hand. "Forgot a coat. Brilliant, huh? I mean, it *is* October."

Nikolai had observed her teetering in the high heels, so when she tripped, he was positioned to catch her. His hand cupped her breast. With an arch smile, Jane gently removed his gloved hand and studied it.

"By the way, what's the deal with the gloves? You're not a germaphobe, are you?"

"No, just protecting the moneymakers." He wiggled his fingers. "Sensitive instruments."

Cleopatra's Needle showed through the foliage on the hill to their right. Nikolai admired the ancient obelisk until the path forked and the two of them walked beneath Greywacke Arch. The moment they were in the shadows, Jane stopped short, pushed him against the cool rock wall, and kissed him.

"Speaking of instruments," she said, pulling away, "I've got one that needs tuning. Why don't you come back to my apartment, see if you can fix it."

"I do have perfect pitch," he said.

———— ♦•◆•♦ ————

Within a week, they were practicing together daily, taking long walks up Riverside Drive to Grant's Tomb, and seeing movies at the theater across from Lincoln Center. And when it came to sex, Jane was even more recklessly rapacious than he, sneaking him into the labyrinthine storage area under the stage before and after rehearsal, pouncing on him in the hallowed symphony reading room, and ambushing him—in his elevator, his laundry room, and, once, in an unoccupied coat check at the Met. Jane, he quickly discovered, concealed a reptilian intensity that only revealed itself during sex; unfortunately, her cello-playing was like her outward personality: bubbly, charming and competent, but hardly transcendent.

Following the opening concerts of the new season, Nikolai was hailed by critics as the next Itzhak Perlman. Nikolai framed the review of a *Times* critic who had previously shredded one of his performances with the Moonlight String Quartet. Recanting, the critic wrote, "*Vernikov radiates a love for the violin so profound, it is as though he has dived into a deep pool, experienced music in its purest form, and returned to share his discoveries. Feeling the notes through Vernikov is tantamount to a religious experience.*"

But then, as quickly as his newfound virtuosity had appeared, it vanished—during a complex Brahms solo. His playing suddenly went limp, and while the audience seemed not to notice, Nikolai did, brooding about it that evening with Jane.

"So you had an off night," she said. "You can't be perfect all the time."

He went to bed pondering this. Killing Vito had imbued him with a previously alien ability to feel deeply, and that evening it drained out of him, leaving him as empty as a blown-out eggshell. Jittery and unable to sleep, Nikolai wandered out to the kitchen and removed a wedge of Jarlsberg from the refrigerator. As he sliced and chewed, he recalled the incident that had started him down this path.

It began as an accident. He was walking out of the 65th Street stage entrance when Vito bumped into him carrying a bag of cement. The impact knocked Nikolai to the sidewalk.

"Hey, watch where you're going, buddy," Vito said.

Nikolai looked up at him. Vito was fatter now and his hairline had receded, but the tell-tale sign of a bully—the simian smirk—was as deeply etched on his face as ever. Still with the cement bag on his shoulder, Vito stepped closer until his head cast a shadow over Nikolai's face.

"Holy shit, I thought you guys went back to Russia."

Nikolai stood up. Vito dropped the cement bag on a pallet.

"Sure left in a hurry," he said. "What happened, your father get caught spying?"

Thick-armed and broad-chested like a silverback gorilla, Vito was still intimidating. He could easily beat Nikolai in a street fight. But deep in the center of his being, Nikolai detected an ash-covered fiery ember, and he knew he wasn't an insecure, frightened child anymore. Mastery of the violin, and the thousands of hours of solitude it entailed, had made him aware of his most secret self and the violent fantasies that resided there. For now, it was better to ignore Vito and leave. Besides, a horse never acknowledges a dog. As Nikolai started down the sidewalk protecting his violin case, Vito called out behind him.

"Guys, come here! I want you to meet my Commie friend."

Nikolai halted, pinched his eyes closed, balled his gloved hands into fists.

"Yeah, that's it, Commie. Turn around."

The temptation was almost overpowering. *No, not here.* Instead he glanced at the watermelons at the corner fruit stand and foresaw how he would extinguish Vito. He looked over his shoulder and smiled.

"Another time." And with that, he walked away.

The cheese was finished. Nikolai ate the final slice and dropped the knife in the sink. Snuffing out Vito had transformed him from a sterile musical contraption into a human being who experienced every note with blinding, soul-searing intensity. He could never go back. Which meant only one thing: he would have to kill again.

For the first few weeks after killing Vito, the new energy had surged through him. He practiced 12 hours a day and spent the rest of the time plucking his new instrument—Jane. More than four hours' sleep was a waste. He was indefatigable; his senses sang. By the sixth and seventh weeks, however, the once overbrimming life force had dissipated to a ghostly fraction of the original, and Nikolai found himself staggering zombie-like to rehearsals and meetings with the Maestro. At this rate, he needed to kill eight people a year to maintain his new level of play. A daunting number, but Nikolai resolved to approach it the same way he did a new score: one measure—or person—at a time. Perhaps mere semantics, but psychologically it made the situation seem manageable.

The second week of November, Nikolai returned to his old Bensonhurst–Bay Ridge neighborhood for one of Vito's co-conspirators, Manny Cardozza. Finding him alone in his garage one night, Nikolai snuck up behind him and with one swipe of a crowbar, snapped his neck like a pretzel stick. Immediately Nikolai's play soared again.

He was fine until the week after Christmas when the extended run of holiday performances had left his body exhausted and his spirit spent. And with six weeks left in the orchestra's season, he knew he wouldn't be able pull it off without an energy boost.

With a soupçon of research Nikolai traced the last of Vito's confederates, Johan Olson, to a remote lake house in the Catskills. He borrowed Jane's girlfriend's SUV and drove through a pre-dawn snowstorm with the menacing first movement of Schubert's Symphony No. 8—the "Unfinished"—blaring on the stereo. When he arrived, he idled partway down the long, secluded driveway, parked and grabbed the claw hammer from his knapsack. He got out and tread stealthily down the drive.

In a stroke of good fortune, Johan was carrying firewood to the house when Nikolai emerged from behind a thick evergreen. It was remarkable how much this Johan resembled the boy version—still with a crew cut, just taller and puffier. He had wanted to strike Johan in the back of the head, but at the last moment the crunching snow gave him away. The moron turned, and the hammer claw splintered Johan's windpipe instead. Perpetually attuned to sound, Nikolai couldn't help noticing the agreeable thunks the logs made as Johan's body collapsed in the snow. Nikolai threw the hammer far into the lake and walked back to the car scuffing out his footprints.

Driving the deserted, snowbound roads back to the interstate, Nikolai lamented at the sloppiness of this one. But even if he left clues, time would be his savior. Time was the key to a perfect murder. Time eroded memory and motive. No one expected a man to harbor thoughts of revenge for over 20 years.

———◆◦◆◦◆———

He was on his way into Robinson's office to discuss bowing, phrasing and tablature for a Bach Easter concert when he overheard the Maestro talking about him on the phone.

"One of the great musical mysteries," the Maestro said. "Sometimes I look at him and can't believe it's the same man. A few months ago, he was just another second violin. Barely heard him, to tell you the truth—what with my brass and clarinets drowning him out back there. At least with that twelve-year-old at Julliard, people saw it coming—the boy had written four *symphonies* already. But this…well, I don't know what to make of it."

Nikolai stood back from the doorway and waited. Across the room, the water cooler gurgled. The Maestro sighed in his office.

"Need to make some changes in the new year, unfortunately. No, not him. My cellos. Weak, I'm afraid. Yes, he's dating one of them. So I've heard. Too bad some of that skill couldn't rub off. Mmm, know what you mean. Something strange afoot, but damned if I have any idea. Well, should ring off now. He'll be popping in any minute."

Nikolai leaned against the wall, caressing his supple leather folio of sheet music. Maestro was suspicious, but there was no way he could know anything, and even if he did, it could prove fortuitous. Killing those mutts had enhanced his playing ten-fold, and Nikolai could only imagine what taking the life of a brilliant conductor would do. He might not need to kill anymore.

Now was too soon, but in a few months the situation would be ripe. All he had to do was hold on.

———◆◆◆———

Out of curiosity Nikolai scanned the newspapers after each murder. The first two appeared in short, back-page Metro pieces, but his killing of Olson was never mentioned. The Catskills were a world away from Manhattan.

Not that he was concerned about being caught. Besides elevating his violin skills, the murders had imbued him with a divine clarity of hindsight and foresight. He had varied his *modus operandi* to prevent the police from detecting a pattern. There were no eyewitnesses and he had always worn his gloves, so there were no fingerprints. Frankly, he was amazed by his ability to anticipate every contingency; if he hadn't been raised a violinist, he might have become a great chess player— another Kasparov, perhaps.

But the Beast in him was not impressed with his inventive plans or their crisp execution. Again and again and again, the Beast demanded fresh blood, and each time the half-life of his creative bliss grew shorter, and he had to kill once more. This was a problem because with each killing he lost another deserving victim, gradually forcing him to lower his standards. Of course there were plenty of people he *wanted* to kill—his building super, whom Nikolai caught poking around in his apartment; a realtor who had lied to him about the apartment's condition and charged him an exorbitant fee; a smug neighbor from the next block who walked his dog to Nikolai's street every morning and let the animal defecate on their sidewalk— yes, there were dozens of these people, but all were sadly off-limits because other people knew he loathed them. His crimes would be traced swiftly back to him.

So Nikolai had to settle for more distant, but no less deserving, victims. In some cases, the killings were purely serendipitous. After a February evening rehearsal that didn't end until one-thirty, a drug addict cornered Nikolai on the stairs of the 66th Street subway entrance, demanding money. Following the briefest of deliberations, Nikolai shoved the addict headlong down the precipitous flight of steps, breaking the man's neck. In March, he fed the Beast a snotty young man he observed stealing a parking space from an old woman. And in early April, while shopping with Jane in the D'Agostino on 91ˢᵗ and Columbus, a drunk businessman bumped into him, causing Nikolai to lose his balance and knock over an apple juice display. The man sneered at Nikolai, who was still in his tux and carrying his violin case, and walked away smiling. Claiming he forgot a score at the rehearsal hall, Nikolai left Jane at the market, followed the man down a dark and snowy Columbus Avenue, and finished him by ramming the point of his Mont Blanc pen into his medulla a few times. The man jerkily tried to turn around. He fell between two parked cars, spasmed and was still. Instantly that luscious creative power welled up inside Nikolai to overflowing; but this time the craving remained.

IV. *Finale: Adagio accelerando; morte dalla vita*

He was at the kitchen table putting the finishing touches on his latest ship-in-a-bottle when his blood-stained tuxedo shirt landed on the table. Nikolai's hand, normally steadier than a brain surgeon's, jerked. His tweezers tore down the ship's mast and rigging.

Jane was leaning against the doorjamb smoking a cigarette, something she never did in the apartment. Maybe it was the harsh light from the kitchen, but her eyes looked dark and puffy.

"Sorry, hon," she said. "Just thought you should know—you're gonna need a new shirt. Couldn't get the stains out of that one."

He did his best to look puzzled. This was how a cheating spouse must feel when caught in a lie.

"*Unbelievable* blood stains," she said. "What'd you do, slaughter a pig?"

Jane blew smoke at the ceiling. She picked lint off her sweater.

"Bad bloody nose," Nikolai said. "You know how dry that rehearsal hall gets."

"Makes sense."

"What do you mean?"

"The stains." She waved the cigarette. "They were mostly on one cuff, like you put your hand up to stop the bleeding."

"That's it, exactly. You'd make a great detective."

Jane nodded, held an imaginary violin under her chin and began to play.

"Practice with me?"

"You look like you need a nap," Nikolai said.

She glared at him. "What I *need* is practice. Are you coming or not?"

"Yes, just let me clean up here."

A moment later the living room resounded with the woody sounds of cello scales. Nikolai bowed his head on the table and softly wept. Jane would want to practice some sprightly piece, no doubt; meanwhile, the tune that pounded in his ears was quite different: the second movement of Beethoven's Third. The funeral march.

The night he had hoped would never come sadly arrived. Jane was meeting her girlfriends at an East Side bar, and Nikolai had ostensibly been invited to a dinner party at the Maestro's (regrettably, his plans for Robinson had to be delayed). He kissed her goodbye next to the umbrella stand, and somberly rode the elevator down. He waited in the alley across from their building. He waited for her.

At quarter to ten she finally emerged, dressed oddly in red Wellies and a shiny red raincoat. It was cool but clear. Her outfit didn't make sense. He dismissed the thought and followed her across Columbus Avenue.

Jane entered Central Park at 79ᵗʰ Street, an act that despite the decline in muggings was strictly *verboten*; one simply didn't walk across the park alone after dark. Nikolai tailed her from 50 yards behind, his throat tightening up every time she skirted a bush or dipped into the shadows. Given what he had in store for her, such worry was absurd. But random attackers, if they chose to kill her, wouldn't do so with restraint and compassion as he soon would. Nikolai, on the other hand, had planned this for a week and devised a painless death for her: a Phillips head screwdriver, sharpened to a point, thrust neatly into her brain stem. He wished it didn't have to be this way—Jane had been a talented, loving and highly sexed companion—but he couldn't risk her exposing his secret.

She passed the Delacorte Theater, where leotard-clad actors would soon be doing Shakespeare in the Park, and across the Great Lawn, where sunbathers would festoon the verdant grass. Continuing down the asphalt path, he was struck by a chilling piece of irony: she was headed straight for the stone arch behind the Met—the place where they had first kissed.

As the path snaked through the trees and descended into a hollow, he lost her. He'd been following her closely, carefully. How could this happen?

It wasn't important right now. In a minute they would be out of the park and his best opportunity for killing her would be gone. Nikolai began to jog. She was still nowhere in sight. He started to run.

Ahead, only the outlines of the archway were visible, and beneath the bridge was a thick pool of gloom. Hopefully rats weren't congregated there; he was scared to death of them.

As he plunged into the darkness, Nikolai observed the lovely acoustics here beneath the bridge. Perhaps one day this summer he would come here to play, to enjoy the coolness and the cave-like echo. Tourists would gather, toss him money and—

Out of the blackness, a glint of something flashed into view. White-hot needles pierced his chest. Had he run into something? A pole? Scaffolding?

Whatever it was, it stole his breath and sent him reeling to the pavement. He scrabbled to his feet, leaned against the rock wall, and slumped down. Where he sat, a faint wash of light from the street lamp shone in and he saw what had happened.

A large knife—his own 12" Henckel's chef's knife, in fact—angled out of his chest like a macabre coat hook. The squeak of rubber boots filled the cavern, and then a shape squatted down in front of him. The smell was unmistakable—it was Jane. His eyes adjusted. She was on her haunches, cupping her chin in black gloves.

"Sorry, baby," she said.

He tried to speak, but she quieted him with a hand on his knee.

"Shhh. You don't have long, so listen."

He had the odd sensation of feeling hot and cold at the same time: the leaking blood, hot on his skin, and his insides, being drained of the blood, like jagged icicles.

"I kept wanting to know—how could this second-stringer develop the talent overnight to become concertmaster? *How?* I had my suspicions, like when you put three hundred miles on Melinda's car in that snowstorm, but it wasn't until the night at D'Agostino's that I *knew*. You see, I followed you. I watched you kill that man, and when I saw your mood and playing the next day, I knew why."

Nikolai shivered. Jane took his hand in hers.

"I had to, Nikolai…you of all people must understand that. The fact is, I've never been more than an above-average cellist. I always wanted to be brilliant, to be a star, but didn't have the talent. I had to, I'm sorry. Maestro threatened to fire me, and my cello is all I have."

She leaned in and kissed him on the mouth.

"Now I'll have your strength." She stood up and looked around. "I really should be getting back. I need to practice. Goodbye, Nikolai."

He watched her fade into the darkness and relished the squeak of her Wellies one last time. And then the part of his brain that had memorized countless pieces of music conjured up the Kreutzer. It was his final lullaby.

THE MAN BEHIND THE SIGNS

Once when I was young and naive, I told my then-colleagues at the Connecticut Department of Transportation that I would never reveal to the public at large that *I* was the author of many of their favorite road signs and slogans. This was back in the mid-70s, when speculation about the identity of Watergate informant Deep Throat was rampant around government water coolers. I was understandably concerned about death threats, stalkers and groupies, not to mention lucrative Madison Avenue job offers. I feared all of these would distract me from my life's purpose: to create clear, authoritative and poetically humorous road signs that increased road safety awareness while reducing traffic fatalities.

After a distinguished but largely anonymous 40-year career, I was content to go to my grave unknown and uncelebrated by the general public. That is, until Deep Throat revealed himself: W. Mark Felt, former Deputy Director of the FBI. That was 2005. Then I read in the paper one morning that Felt had died. Sipping a cup of coffee, I nodded and said to myself, "It's time."

My work as a Senior Road Sign Engineer came about from necessity. I was 10 years old, and the family farm in upstate Rhinebeck, NY was in trouble. Before WWII, we had always been able to count on sales from our vegetable stand to carry us through the winter, but after the war, Route 9 gradually diverted all traffic away from dirt roads like ours. So with nothing but some paint, old plywood and my Radio Flyer wagon, I set up a series of dandy couplets to draw traffic to our stand. That first Friday evening, we sold out of everything, the Manhattan weekenders skidding into the sandy lot and jostling each other to get the last zucchini, tomato, eggplant. The couplets were corny, but this may explain why they were so effective:

So, you're up from the City
And sitting pretty.

You've got burgers and steaks
And ice cream for shakes.

But you don't have sweet corn,
Nor tomatoes, nor cukes...

So, take your next right and go to Duke's!

DUKE FAMILY FARM STAND
8 a.m. – 7p.m., 7 Days
Vegs. — Berries — Fall Apple Cider
Next Right — ½ mile

Of course, like all sign makers and craftsmen of the compact, memorable message, I had always admired the Burma Shave technique of carrying the message across a quarter-mile on multiple pieces of signage, and my own farm stand series clearly shows the Burma Shave influence. However experience has taught me that this approach is cumbersome and, more important, *dangerous* on road work sites, where the loss of a single placard renders your message insensible and distracting, and a motorist's sudden braking can cause the very accidents the signs are supposed to prevent.

Over many long nights in the Sign Engineering Lab my capable associate Millicent Parker and I tested various paint types, color schemes, metal compositions and text contrasts, not to mention increasingly omnipresent iconography. One of our breakthroughs occurred in 1971, when Millicent, a Cambridge University linguist, determined that the compact, rhythmic couplet, whether rhymed or not, was the ideal form for a road sign message—a technique I employed in one of my catchiest road safety slogans:

LET 'EM WORK,
LET 'EM LIVE!

Codenamed *SISYPHUS* during development, *"Let 'em work, Let 'em live!"* is infamous among road sign engineers because it was simultaneously invented by myself and a South Carolina man who shall remain nameless. Like Newton and Leibniz, simultaneous discoverers of the calculus, my nemesis and I each came up with the slogan in the early 70s, but it wasn't until the public's collective cynicism spiked after Vietnam and Watergate that they were ready for such a macabrely ironical message. My version went out in time for the 1977 summer construction season; his not until the winter of the following year.

Unfortunately, in this business it's all about being first, which is why I won the Roadway Safety Alliance

Award of 1978 and was featured on the covers of *Road Crew Digest* and *Going Places!* magazines while the South Carolinian remained in obscurity. In 1980 he filed suit, claiming I had stolen the idea, but when it was proved in U.S. District Court that I had never been to his state, much less knew anyone there, he dropped it.

Last year we met at an American Society of Civil Engineers conference, where I was the keynote speaker. Hired to deliver a speech about *"Let 'em work, Let 'em live!"* I was fully prepared to acknowledge the man from SC and declare that we had simultaneously and independently conceived of the campaign (something fairly common in the worlds of science and engineering). But when I attempted to shake his hand during the meet-and-greet cocktail hour and he snubbed me, I decided to crush him once and for all. I ran onstage like a motivational speaker and said, "Hello, I'm Alfred Duke. Come on, everybody, say it with me!" I stretched out my hands. *"Let 'em work, let 'em live!"*

The South Carolina man hastened out of the ballroom; rumor was, with tears in his eyes.

———————◆•◆•◆———————

There are a few great slogans out there for which, while not the creator, I was the catalyst. One was for New York State. Just as Nobel Prize-winning Physicist Richard Feynman did during the Congressional hearings on the Challenger disaster, through the right questions and a vivid demonstration I helped New York create a memorable slogan.

It was Christmas Eve in Albany and snowing hard. We'd been at it for three days, and we had to get the slogan to the sign makers if we wanted the signage in time for the summer construction season. The engineers had just finished a tangential, though no less heated, argument over fixed steel guardrails vs. portable concrete Jersey barriers, and the air in the room was silver with cigarette smoke. It was up to me to break the impasse.

"Gentlemen…ladies," I said, winking at Millicent, "I think we're getting off-topic. I want you to forget everything else and ask yourselves, 'What can we do to prevent *this* from happening?'"

Before they could see what I was holding, I took the toy car and whisked it down the conference table so it plowed through the model construction site, mowing down the toy workers, scattering them to the floor. No one spoke. The radiator pinged.

"Now," I said, "what is it you want motorists to do?"

"We want them to slow down, use their brakes."

Another engineer leaned back in his chair, tented his fingers and gazed at the ceiling tiles.

"It's like, 'Hey, take it easy, we're trying to make a living over here…not so fast…give us a break.'"

"That's it," the first one said. "Give 'em a brake!"

Millicent and I smiled at each other. We stood up.

"Gentlemen," I said, "our work here is done. Drive safely."

Before I became a full-time freelancer, for several years I moonlighted for other states' DOT, including Vermont's.

They were having problems with speeders in a work zone on Route 2 near Cabot. It was 1984, and a certain celebrity who lived in the area had just won the Pulitzer Prize for Drama. The slogan I concocted was a stretch, with the need for a particular rhyme limiting my options:

> *It's a Work Zone, dammit!*
> *Don't tear through here like David Mamet!*

I dismissed the idea. I had no tangible evidence of Mr. Mamet's lead-footedness. Besides, I enjoyed his *Glengarry Glen Ross* and didn't want to libel him. Millicent hated the slogan, citing the dubious dramaturgical literacy of work zone speeders.

"And it's *reaching*, Alfred," she said. "You're so obviously trying for the laugh."

She was right, of course. Terribly blocked that winter and unable to retrofit any of my previous ideas, I returned the advance check.

Three years later, I was back on top, cranking out great work for Pennsylvania's "We're Serious About Truck Safety" program (known sarcastically in the industry as the S.T.F.D., or Slow The Fuck Down, project). One of the program's campaigns—a guerilla one targeted at long-haul truckers—included a curt message on stickers above rest stop urinals:

> *Stop now and sleep, O tired trucker…*
> *Before you crash and the cops say, "You dumb fucker."*

From the moment it debuted, the slogan was reviled by the trucking community. While relieving myself in a rest stop bathroom outside Harrisburg, a pair of truckers flanking me discussed the sign.

"Boy," one said, "I ever find the guy that wrote this shit, know what I'm gonna do?"

His buddy flushed his urinal. "No, what?"

"I'm gonna cut his damn prick off, that's what."

Suddenly nauseous, I finished quickly and left without flushing.

Then the great state of Texas called. They wanted something folksy, yet hard-assed. One night for inspiration, Millicent and I put some Mac Davis records on the turntable and drank a bottle of Garrison Brothers Texas Straight Bourbon Whiskey. When I woke up, my head felt like a cleaved piece of mesquite as I fumbled around for a pencil. I had a gem, and I knew it:

A ticket in these parts'll cost you plenty,
But hit a feller and you'll get 20.

While initially reluctant about using the informal contraction of "parts'll" for "parts will," not to mention the obvious regionalism of "feller," I'm pleased with how I managed to communicate the serious consequences of work zone speeding in a sprightly, jovial tone.

As Millicent often observed, rhymed couplets like "plenty/twenty" are among the most easily memorized word packages there are, making them extremely effective for conveying rules and regulations. They are also known for their aphrodisiacal properties, which may explain Andrew Marvell's use of them in "To His Coy Mistress," a poem that, when the office cleared out, I frequently recited to Millicent as she poured her second cup of chamomile:

Had we world enough and time,
This coyness lady were no crime...

By the time I got to *"Now therefore, while the youthful hue / Sits on thy skin like morning dew,"* her blouse was off, her brassiere about to be. She shook her hair out and talked dirty to me, something that is pleasantly startling to hear from a seemingly prim girl of the London suburbs.

"Mmm, say it, Alfred, say it! Word-fuck me, you sign god!"

Swiping our sketches, photographs and reference books to the floor, she crawled atop the long steel lab table and bade me join her, looking at me while lightly brushing her inner thighs. In the early days she wore a garter belt and stockings, and the mere sight of her—a smile peeking through a curtain of hair, arms widely beckoning, breasts heaving, toes wiggling—was so arousing that I had to think of something else as I mounted her. Some men allegedly use baseball stats, like team members and their positions. I ran through a mental checklist of the W-Series traffic warning signs: *"W1... Turn and Curve... W2...Intersection...W5...Width Restriction...W20 and 21...my specialties...Work Zone and Road Work...W24... Double Reverse Curve..."* If Millicent were still doing dirty-talk, I wouldn't make it through the list once; but when she was quiet and soft and submissive, I could abandon my litany and focus on the woman I loved.

Which reminds me. One of my signs, "SPEED HUMP," became a Federal DOT standard. You've no doubt seen it while driving through residential developments or business parks, and perhaps you've even remarked to yourself, "Why speed *hump* and not speed *bump*?" Well, I'll tell you. In the summer of 1969, when I was assigned the project, Millicent, fresh from Cambridge across the pond, with bouffant hair, miniskirts and knee-high Nancy Sinatra boots, was hired by Connecticut DOT as a linguist and junior road sign engineer. We were intoxicated with each other from the start (Millicent was 22 at the time; I was 30). Most afternoons, she'd burst into the lab, throw her back against the door and lock it.

"I need a proper shagging. Fancy a hump, Alfred?"

Pretending to check my watch, I'd say, "Hmm… a hump? All right, but we'd better make it speedy."

Thus, SPEED HUMP. To this day, Millicent and I get a good chuckle out of that one.

In the 90s, when transportation sign design was being taken over by the graphic designers, the universal signs movement, and the AIGA 50 symbols crowd, I began to think about retirement. I didn't like their militant agenda of forcing sign designers to accommodate the illiterate. In my opinion, if a person can't read, he has no business driving a car. Pictures have their place, certainly, and I know the theory—that a single visual icon can take the place of dozens of words—but that only works for simplistic ideas like "Beware of falling rocks." Icons are soulless and witless, and can't communicate shades of meaning the way a well-crafted couplet can. I and other traditionalists resisted the trend as long as we could, but it was clear that the icon lovers were going to win. I had a brief comeback when the United Nations contracted me for a slogan to improve global road safety. I came up with the internationally acclaimed "Road Safety is No Accident," but since it debuted the same year Millicent and I retired to Key West, its popularity came too late to help my ailing career.

For a while we scuba-dived, gardened and played a good deal of tennis, but after decades of 10- to 12-hour days doing work we loved, a life of leisure quickly became unbearable. We drank. We argued—once, in the backyard of Hemingway's house.

In a loud whisper, with one of the six-toed cats rubbing against our legs, Millicent suddenly started ranting about how she had never wanted to retire, saying for the first time things like, "What the hell am I doing with a man your age, anyway? I'd still be working right now, were it not for you!" Deeply hurt, I holed up at a friend's until Millicent tracked me down two days later. Rain dripped from the palm trees on the patio.

"Oh, Alfred," she said, "I miss it. What are we going to do?"

I hugged her. She was still a fox, but a silver-haired one now.

Staring over her shoulder at the ocean, I said, "I don't know, Milly, I don't know."

———◆◆◆———

Then an interesting thing happened. Traffic engineers, looking for ways to better control traffic flow on major corridors, rediscovered the power of textual signs, this time using giant LCD screens on overpasses. They needed old-school sign engineers like Millicent and me to write the messages that would be read by thousands of backed-up, late and angry drivers.

Besides an ocean view, our Key West bungalow has a state-of-the-art traffic control center. In a nondescript shed out back, a team of six in three shifts monitors 106 locations along all major U.S. traffic corridors. The moment an accident occurs, or if we spot an unexplained slowdown, we gather data, alert local authorities and write messages that will inform and hopefully mollify motorists.

Millicent and I enjoy this new work because it has allowed us to mentor the next generation of sign engineers. One of them, a young Cuban American woman, shows great promise; she was recently nominated for a AAA Travelers' Guardian Angels Award (or AAATGAA). It's comforting to know she'll be here, continuing the tradition after we're gone.

So, the next time you're bumper-to-bumper on the Beltway, the L.I.E., the I-5 in L.A. or even Route 1 heading to Key West, and you read a quippy and informative traffic flash, think of us.

We do this because we love it, but we also do it for you.

To keep you and your family safe.

Happy motoring.

THE BOOTLEGGER

You live on an island off the coast of Maine. You have six children by three women, one of the women being your current wife. You live in a small Cape that you built yourself because you are a very handy man and have worn many hats: carpenter, cooper, logger, fisherman, and stonecutter. Driving your rust-mottled truck around the spruce and granite island, you often tell yourself that you are a handy man capable of great things. You keep telling yourself this.

You drink a lot of homemade beer in the small addition you put on five years ago. Every man needs a place to admire souvenirs from his adventures. Take the Indian rug on the floor over there. A genuine Passamaquoddy guide gave you that rug while on a hunting trip. On your desk is a photograph of the Indian and you standing in front of a cabin next to the bear you shot. That bearskin now guards the entrance to the room. Your children tread over it with muddy feet sometimes, unaware of how few men there are who have taken a bear and have the skin to prove it.

It's 1931, and you and your friends are unemployed. Three times, you went to the mainland to scrounge up work in the concrete factories and forests there. For a while, you had a job in a logging camp out in Jackman. Did everything from cutting the big pines to riding them downstream because you're a handy man. Worked your way up to foreman of a truck crew that drove into the deep woods, where the roads were nothing but sucking, mean mud. Occasionally, when you got stuck, logs toppled off, and a couple times you were yelled at by the mill manager for being under-loaded.

One night when you drove back into camp, you were so drunk you had to have one of the other men shift gears for you. When you got out, the mill manager was there, yelling and waving his pencil and clipboard at you, so you cracked him between the eyes with your fist. A fist made big from years of manual labor when you really had wanted to become a doctor. His nose bone split, blood gushed, and as soon as he regained consciousness, you were fired.

After a month-long bender somewhere in the North Country, you came home and had to listen to your wife bitch about you being canned, how there wasn't enough money, and that your youngest son needed new boots. His socks stuck out of the holes in his boots, and other children teased him for this. So you taught him to fight, to beat up any boy who made fun of him or his sisters for not having much. You didn't have the money to buy new boots then, and it's unlikely you'll have it anytime soon.

So here you are, unemployed and drunk, with three kids and a wife in a tiny Cape on a small island fifteen miles off the coast of Maine, and three more kids on the mainland. You've drunk so much beer, it hurts to lift yourself out of the chair and walk outside to piss on the woodpile. You like pissing on the woodpile—after all, it's your woodpile.

Sometimes you grab your Smith & Wesson .44 Special out of the drawer beneath the whale oil lamp and slip it in your pocket on your way outside. You shoot at a target on the broad side of the shed. Even drunk you're a good shot, and once you were jailed for a week on the mainland for shooting a man. It wasn't your fault, though; the sawed-off Greek son-of-a-bitch pulled a knife on you in a tavern.

"I gotta da knife," he gibbered, flashing the blade around.

He thought he was tough, so you reached in your coat pocket and pulled out your trusty .44 Special.

"I gotta da pistol," you gibbered in reply before plugging him above his collarbone.

When the sheriff claimed you were trying to murder the bastard, you told him you hit him exactly where you'd aimed and knew there was no danger of killing him—he had a lot of meat above his collarbone.

There are a lot of things in your life that you regret, but shooting that prick isn't one of them. Besides, someone once told you that you regret the things you *don't* do, not the things you do. You always liked that saying.

———◆———

You slip on your overcoat and felt fedora and walk, head tucked into your chest, over to Trevor Boyle's fishing shack. The two of you sit on chairs beside a potbelly coal stove and drink home brew you stashed here a few months ago. Trevor cuts slices from a stick of hard salami and eats them straight off the blade. With the waves smashing the rocks outside, you feel like hell about your life and know you need to find some way of making money. Eventually you'll come up with a good idea. You always do.

Trevor puts down the salami and opens his mouth to speak, but instead of words coming out, his voice just squeaks at first, like a steam engine getting warmed up. This trait of his has always annoyed you, but since he's your friend, you ignore it.

"Stinks having to hole up like this, don't it?" he says.

"Yup."

"Wish the taverns were open again." He sips his beer. "How's the fire?"

"Fine," you say. "You got the draw just right."

Trevor smiles at this. He polishes off his bottle, reaches deep into the ice bucket and fishes out another. Water trickles down the sides, and Trevor shakes his hand at the stove. The stove hisses.

"Man can't get a drink these days," he says. "Have to spend a fortune for a little shot in one of the speaks or hide in here like some kind of leper. It's inhuman, I'm telling you."

Trevor's words are far off somewhere, mixed up in the warmth of the beer. You stare out the grimy window at the sea. Winter's moving in early. It's barely October and the dank, miserable weather that the summer people never see has already begun. The island is barren much of the time, the fishermen and lobstermen staying indoors to repair their nets and traps. Lately, you and Trevor have spent many afternoons in the shack listening to the foghorn bellow from across the island.

The sea is rough now, and only the foolish fishermen still dare the waves. A while back your brother died and left you a forty-foot scallop trawler named *Elizabeth*. She's what you'd call "seasoned," but you only take her out in the spring and summer. About a month ago, you dry-docked her down at Pung's wharf. Letting your mind wander, you think of the beer and your boat, the sea and your son's boots. You're about to reach for another bottle when the idea hits you like a falling tree.

"Trevor," you announce proudly, "I've got an idea."

He is sloppy drunk, nearly falling out of his chair. His boots are starting to burn where he has them propped up against the stove, so you knock them off.

"What?" Trevor's bottle is clutched to his chest. Some of the brew spills on his shirt.

"By Jesus, I've got an idea," you say.

At this point, Trevor notices his smoking boots. He snatches the pot of old coffee from the stove, stumbles outside, and dumps the hideous liquid on the soles.

"Shoot," he says. "Ruined 'em."

"Forget the boots. Now listen." You stand up and start pacing between the stove and the Army cot.

"What are you talking about?"

"We're gonna run whiskey, Trevor. We'll use my boat, run up to New Brunswick, and bring back whiskey. We'll make a fortune."

Trevor shakes his head. He's using his jackknife to cut the warped rubber off his boot soles.

"Yeah, but you're forgetting something." He points the knife at you. "They've got patrols out everywhere. They're checking boats from Eastport all the way down to Kittery. How in hell we gonna get a boatload of Canadian whiskey by them inspectors?"

You aren't sure about this yet, but you don't want Trevor's objections to dampen your enthusiasm.

"You'll see," you say.

———————⟡———————

Turns out that Trevor doesn't need much convincing. Half an hour later, you send him away with a pat on the back and instructions to sober up and pack some things. The two of you will meet at Bobby Oakes's in the morning for breakfast. In the meantime, you walk down to the wharf and ask Pung Eye to put your boat in. Naturally he's curious, so you tell him you're going to do a little fishing. But he knows you better than this. In high school, you always had a scheme. Once, you and Trevor stole an old timer's sloop and followed two girls and their parents back to Boston. You were gone for a month. Pung winks at you now with his good eye.

To put your plan into action, you need some cash, some working capital. Of course, you don't have any money at the moment, but this has never stopped you. There are a few fellas around who owe you, so it's time to collect.

You drive to the north end of the island, park the truck, and hop on Guptill's ferry to cross the Thoroughfare to North Haven. A famous painter, name of Burke, lives over there. Rumor is, Burke was good friends with N.C. Wyeth as a boy. A couple years back, you fixed the roof on Burke's studio, but he didn't have the cash to pay you, so you let it go saying you'd be back someday to get it. Well, today is the day.

The sounds of a trumpet—Satchmo would be your guess—are blaring out of the studio windows when you arrive. The weeds around the door are brown and brittle and scrape your knees as you climb the steps. Out of courtesy, you knock before stepping inside. Sure enough, Burke is there, wearing overalls without a shirt, painting a nude teenage girl draped with a fishing net. The girl glances at you, lets out a little huff, and wiggles back into the sofa. She's one of those girls you have to work at keeping your eyes off. Five minutes go by before Burke finally opens his fat trap.

"What do you want?"

"Burke," you say, "I fixed your roof a couple years back. I need the money you owe me."

"What roof?"

"This roof," you say, jutting your chin at the ceiling. "You couldn't pay me then, so I said I'd come back. I need my money now."

"No money," Burke says. "Take a painting. Got plenty of those."

"Won't do, Burke," you say. "I need the greenbacks."

"Listen here, take a painting or get the hell out. I'm losing light."

He waves his brush at the stack of canvases leaning against the far wall. You'd take one of his paintings, but art's a tough sell and you need cash, today. The phonograph gets your attention as a possible trade, but it's seen better days. Besides, it's on a table beside the sofa, which leads you to believe it's part of the painting Burke's doing. Desperate to get your money and leave, you scan the studio for something of value and your eyes fall upon an antique clock—worth maybe fifty dollars to a dealer—and a gold pocket watch beside it. You step across to the desk and take them.

"Hey!"

"Simmer down, Burke, before you get hurt."

"Those were my father's."

"Not anymore." You start for the door.

For an overweight artist, Burke is surprisingly quick and catches you off guard when he throws his stool at you and hits you in the back. But the stool doesn't break like it does in the radio shows; it only makes you mad. You march over to him, pinch his nose in your fingers and force him to the ground. He is sniveling on the studio floor when the blood begins to run. As you leave, the girl lets out a sigh and the door bangs behind you.

———————⋅◆⋅———————

On the mainland, you and Trevor trade in the timepieces. You'd like to get eighty bucks for the two, but the white-haired dealer with the perpetual stoop remembers you from a bad trade in the past. He slaps forty dollars into your empty palm and waves you toward the door. You want to argue, but you can tell by the way he looks up at you with one eye tightly squinted that he won't be had again; and, there are no other dealers in town. You shouldn't have been dishonest the first time, you tell yourself as Trevor joins you on the street, but you can't help it—it's in you.

At the diner, you sit at the counter and wag your eyebrows at the redheaded waitress, Holly. She's a keen woman with lots of wit, and a fiery minx in the sack. You know this because just about every time you're in town, you go into the diner for coffee and to ask her when she gets off. She replies, "Whenever you'll make me." The two of you then hustle down to the Fair Seas Inn and have a thunderstorm beneath the crisp, starched sheets. You consider asking Holly now when she gets off, but with Trevor sipping coffee beside you it's not a good idea.

"Hiya, darlin'," you say.

She refills your cup, slowly, letting the coffee run over a little.

"Hiya, baby." She pushes some stray hair away from her face. "Wanna know when I get off?"

"Sorry, darlin'." You point at Trevor with your finger against your chest. "Can't. Need to talk to Joe. He in?"

She sighs. "Yeah, I'll get him." You feel her gaze on your face until she disappears behind the double doors into the kitchen, where Joe is.

———— ◆◆◆ ————

You and Trevor take a corner table with Joe and ask him if anyone wants some whiskey. You're making a run to Canada, you tell him, and you're taking orders.

"I'll take a barrel," he says. "Keep it in the basement. Anybody wants a nip, I'll have it."

"Anyone else?"

"Lemme call around."

So you sit, and wait, and fester over how fine Holly looks today, her breasts snug in the tight navy dress she wears in the diner. While Joe makes his calls from the phone booth in the back, you sense the sullen eyes of every man in the place on the back of your neck. Finally, Joe hangs up and pulls the phone booth door open. As he approaches you, he hauls up his belt, which, on its last notch, is fighting a losing battle. He tells you that Frank, owner of the hardware store, wants one barrel; and Al, owner of the bank and publisher of the newspaper, wants two.

"You know," Joe says, "this is risky business. I hope you boys know what you're doing."

You open your coat enough for Joe to see the revolver. Trevor grins and looks around.

"We've got it covered. Now, about the money."

Setting out in choppy seas, the two of you keep the trawler close to shore. With the onset of winter, the currents shift, and before you know it you can be dashed against a rock, blown onto a sandbar, or carried out to deep water. Each time the bow slices a wave, the boat lurches and spray flies up on the windshield. The two of you take turns walking up to the bow to de-ice the wipers.

You're headed northeast toward Blacks Harbor. Trevor and you take turns at the wheel and snatch naps in the forward berth. Before you left the mainland, Trevor stowed plenty of beans and biscuits, coffee and water, and most of the time you eat in the cabin, anchored in coves. Once in a while, though, Trevor talks you into going on the mainland for a real meal of haddock chowder or fried scallops.

You pass Bar Harbor and gas up again in Jonesport. In clear weather, which you consider a good omen, you break for the open sea and skirt North Head on Grand Mahan Island. Soon, the clanging channel markers with their seagull sentries become scarce. The mainland is nothing but a purple mist to your left. Blacks Harbor is just hours away.

———◆•◆•◆———

The morning after you arrive, you awake in your room at the inn with gray light sifting through chinks in the blinds. You grunt, scratch your ass, and roll out of bed to the window. Hordes of shifty, unshaven men with rumpled clothes welded to their skin stir in the square below your window. Across the square, down at the wharf, Elizabeth bobs contentedly in her slip.

Dressed, shaved, and full with eggs and fishcakes, you and Trevor head out to find whiskey. The air is rich with the smell of smokehouses and the chatter of fellow schemers. You stop in two stores, a trading post and a pharmacist, and ask the proprietors, but they just shake their heads from behind their counters. For the first time since you hatched this plot, you feel a slight knot in your stomach. You wonder if you can pull this off.

At the haberdashery, you ask a young man the same question as you look at the price tag on a heavy wool overcoat. You'd like to buy it for your oldest son at college on a scholarship. All the girls would fawn over him, the chip off the old block. The young man glances past you at the street and motions toward the back.

"Come back here with me," he says. "I think I have just what you need."

"I don't want the coat right now," you say.

For a second, the young man in his spectacles reminds you of the mill manager whose nose you wrecked, but the two of you follow him into the back room anyway, where he closes the door.

"You can't shout that around here. There are Customs agents all over the place." He pulls a cigarette out of his breast pocket and lights it. "They wait around town to see who is bootlegging and arrest them at sea."

"Damn," Trevor says, behind you.

"That's not all of it." He exhales a stream of smoke through his nose. "There are lot of drifters and amateur pirates around. You could get robbed."

Trevor nudges your arm. "Maybe we shouldn't bother."

You consider giving up, not taking the risk, but then you think of the shack where you and Trevor drink, the grime on the windows, your wife angry about not having any money, and you know you have to do it. Others might get caught, but you have a plan. You are clever and handy and can do what other men can't.

"Look, we've come a long way." You hand the salesman five dollars. "Where can we get some whiskey?"

"If you're really serious, I will contact the right man and have him meet you where you are staying."

"We're serious."

"Are you staying at the inn?"

You nod. "Room number five."

"Fine." he says. "Go back there and wait. He will knock five times."

"What's this guy's name?" Trevor asks.

"Jean."

"Put that thing away," Trevor says.

You have the .44 out and aimed at the dressing mirror. The two of you are sitting in high-backed leather chairs in opposite corners of the hotel room, facing the door. After three hours waiting for this Jean, your ass is cramping up, and now you doubt he'll show.

"I'm not going to shoot anything," you say. "I'm just bored."

"Well, you're not gonna make much of an impression on this Jean fella waving that thing around."

You slip the gun into the bookcase beside you, where you can grab it easily if there's trouble. Finally, the five knocks come. You think there were five, but you can't be sure because you were dozing.

"Trevor, how many was that?"

"I'm not sure," he says.

You put your hand on the pistol. "Come in."

The door opens and a slim man with a scant mustache walks in backwards, wheeling a cart.

"Hey," Trevor says, "we didn't order any room service."

The man clicks the door shut and eases the cart to one side.

"I am Jean." His back is perfectly straight as he speaks. "Let's talk whiskey now, shall we?"

This Jean moves gracefully—like a magician you saw once in Portland. With a wave of his hand, he yanks a napkin off a bread basket, and out of the rising steam produces a heavy flask.

"You would like a sample, no?"

You smile broadly and let go of the gun.

———————◆•◆•◆———————

After a few drinks, Jean tells you that if you wait a day, he will get hold of six barrels of fine Canadian whiskey for you and have them delivered to your boat in the night. He then raises his jigger for a toast, and a chill creeps across your shoulders. Something tells you he has rehearsed this many times before.

"To the two of you," he says, "the bootleggers!"

You throw the whiskey back. It runs down your throat cool at first, then burns a little, just the way it should.

With a few more samples of the product, your suspicion subsides, and you and Trevor become pals with this mysterious man with the pencil-thin mustache. He came to New Brunswick from Montreal when he was 14, and now and then he forgets himself and blurts out something in French, which you do not understand. The only French you ever heard was out of the mouth of a petite, blonde kitten from Quebec City you bedded one night in a cathouse near the logging camp. She cried out something in French while you humped away at her.

You tell Jean how you plan to smuggle the whiskey back to Maine. You'll store the barrels on deck, wrapped in a net, and covered by a tarp. The barrels, you explain, should be filled so there is no air left in them and have lead plates bolted to the bottoms. That way, if you or Trevor spot a patrol, you can heave the entire net overboard and the barrels will sink just below the surface, where they'll be invisible to the inspectors. The cable will be connected to the net and the base of the stern, so they can search the boat for smuggled liquor all they want, but won't find anything. Then, once the inspectors leave, you and Trevor can hook the cable up to the winch and haul the barrels back in.

You hoist another drink up to your mouth and slide it down. Jean says you are brilliant, that he has known many bootleggers but you are by far the cleverest. Trevor agrees with a hearty nod.

Heading back the first day, around dusk, Trevor yells to you that a ship is approaching, maybe U.S. Coast Guard. He passes you the binoculars. Sure enough, a cutter rolls with the waves maybe two miles behind. You come about so the bow faces the cutter and they won't be able to see what you're doing. Together you and Trevor tear the tarp off the netted barrels and check the cable at the focal point of the net. Everything is secure. The barrels are heavy—a couple hundred pounds a piece—so you have to jack them toward the water, one by one, with an iron post-digger you brought. Once the majority of them reach the edge of the deck, the whole net topples into the water like a sack of cement. You check the eye hook where the cable connects to the stern. All set. Straining your eyes, you can just make out the net with the barrels hovering about ten feet under the murky green water. The plan is perfect, you clever, handy man.

The cutter pulls alongside, and a dinghy is lowered. A lieutenant climbs into the boat with a burly enlisted man, who begins rowing. They pull to.

"We're coming aboard," the officer says.

The enlisted man tosses you a rope.

"What for?"

"Standard search of your vessel," he says. "We're stopping all boats your size that pass through these waters."

"Help yourself," you say.

"Coffee?" Trevor blows steam off a tin cup, raises it at the lieutenant. "Just made a fresh pot."

"No, thanks."

They lift the engine door on the deck. They rifle the lockers in the cabin. They poke around in the forward berth, where you and Trevor take turns napping. They find nothing. As they speed away, you and Trevor wave.

"Coffee?" you say to Trevor.

"Thought it'd be a nice touch."

You shake your head and grin. Sometimes you really like this friend of yours.

———————◆———————

When you arrive in Rockland with the barrels, Joe is impressed and immediately contracts you for five more. Back on the island, you give your wife a fat envelope of money for the house, and she kisses you and leads you by your belt into the bedroom, where you tumble together for a couple hours. Your youngest son gets new boots, and so does Trevor. After three more voyages to Blacks Harbor, you and Trevor are each a thousand dollars richer. You share your wealth with the mothers of your children on the mainland, pulling your boat into the harbor in the thick of night, and arriving at their doors with armfuls of gifts. For your oldest son, the one at college, you buy that wool overcoat you saw in the haberdashery.

Business, to put it mildly, is good.

More and more folks want your bootlegged whiskey, including the sheriff, and now when you step into the diner in Rockland, everyone hushes. For Holly you buy a red bustier and matching garters. She loves the gift and shows her appreciation by shimmying out of the undergarments as soon as she gets into them. In your room at the Fair Seas, she takes another swig from the bottle and climbs back on top of you. You are beginning to truly enjoy bootlegging.

By the sixth run, your operation has increased to a dozen barrels per trip. Sometimes you and Trevor have to dump the load overboard three or four times during a voyage. It's a nuisance, but worth it when the cash arrives.

The evening before the seventh run, you and Trevor meet Jean in his office behind the herring cannery. The sour, heady odor is enough to make you faint.

"The whiskey is aboard," Jean reports.

"Who's guarding the boat tonight?" you ask.

"René."

"Good." You pay Jean for the extra large order: eighteen barrels.

"And here," you say, handing him a $100 bill. "For you."

"What is this? I do not want your money."

"Maybe not, but you're taking it. We couldn't have done this without you."

"Thank you." He slips the bill into his shoe. "And now, let me ask you, how is the system working, using the net and winch?"

"Fine."

"Good, good. And have you been following the coast or staying out to sea?"

"Coast," Trevor says. "Takes longer, but we know it better."

"Very good," Jean says, leaning back in his chair. "Squalls can blow up quickly this time of year."

"We know. You forget, Jean, we grew up on an island."

"Yes, I forget. Well, goodbye my friends."

"Goodbye, Jean." You shake hands and step out into the night.

In the morning, you and Trevor rise early and take breakfast in the hotel dining room. Despite all of your trips, this is the first time you've been in here. You relish the softness of the cushion against your sore back and the warmth of the fire across the room. Outside, the sun is just about to rise. The horizon is a deep orange, nearly red on the water beyond the boats swaying in the harbor.

"Look, Trevor. Some pretty, ain't it?"

Trevor takes a bite of sausage. "Sure is, but there's a saying about that. 'Red in the morning, sailors take warning. Red at night, sailor's delight.' Maybe we should wait till tomorrow."

You shake your head. "No way. The boat's loaded."

"Seems to me waiting a day wouldn't hurt us any." Trevor pokes at his flapjacks.

"We'll be fine. We can sit easy after this one."

Chugging out of the harbor, you are greeted by the flattest sea and the clearest sky you've ever seen. It's brisk on the water, and the salt hangs thick in the air, like it's frozen. After spending the last couple days around all the finery of the hotel, the roughness of the unpainted wheel is welcome in your calloused hands.

"Eighteen barrels, Trevor. Lot of money."

"Think I'm gonna buy a new truck in the spring," Trevor says.

You laugh. Trevor is easily satisfied. You, on the other hand, want to take the couple of thousand you've made and parlay it into more money. You're not sure how yet, but you're a handy man and will come up with something.

"Hey, take a look at this," Trevor says. "That's no cutter."

Trevor takes the helm and hands you the binoculars.

"Looks like a lobster boat," you say.

"Think it could be some of those pirates that kid in the haberdashery was telling us about?"

"Maybe."

You slide the .44 out of your jacket, break it open and check the cylinder. Six shells. For all your talk about being ready for trouble, you forgot to bring extra bullets. You tuck the pistol in the netting, under some dry kelp atop one of the barrels.

"We're gonna let them board us," you say.

"What!"

"We can't outrun them, Trevor," you say. "We're too loaded down. When they get close, lift up the engine door and pour some water in there."

"Oh, I get you." He smiles.

The unknown craft grows on the horizon. Studying the boat through the binoculars, you make out three men, but they are too far away to see clearly.

"Okay, Trevor, pour it in."

Steam rises out of the engine compartment, and you and Trevor start waving your arms in distress. You are a clever man, you tell yourself. The approaching boat will think your engine is dead, and they'll board expecting no resistance. They probably won't be armed either. But you will.

"They're pulling to," Trevor says. "Hey, wait a minute. Isn't that Jean?"

It is Jean. He stands on the deck with one foot propped up on a crate. You turn to Trevor.

"Let him and one of the other guys on board," you say. "Show them the engine. Remember, play like it's dead."

"Gotcha."

"My friends, what is wrong?" Jean calls.

"Engine's gone," you say. "Can we put the whiskey on your boat?"

"Of course. We will be right over to help."

Jean and a big man with one arm stand near the edge of the boat as the pilot brings their boat alongside yours. The right sleeve of the big man's Navy pea coat flops around in the stiffening breeze. You haven't noticed until now, but the wind is picking up something fierce. You reach out, grab Jean's wrist, and haul him aboard.

"Merci," he says.

You think of the pistol back in the net and can't wait to get to it.

"Tell you what," you say. "Why don't you guys see if you can get this thing started. I'll get the barrels ready to load."

You walk over to the net. Trevor is pointing into the engine hatch, and Jean and the one-armed man are peering in. You check the pilot of their boat. He's at the wheel, reading a newspaper. All that practice against the shed is about to pay off. The newspaper the pilot is reading is the perfect sized target, and about as far away as your shed is from the woodpile. You slip the gun out, crouch behind the net, and take aim.

You fire. With the crack of the gun, Jean and One-Arm whip around, but it is too late; the pilot is slumped over in his seat with the newspaper inches from his face, like he's still reading it. You hold the gun on Jean.

"What is this?" he says, his eyes darting around. "You just shot an innocent man."

"You're a thief. You came here to rob us."

"What are you talking about? A storm is blowing up. We were trying to warn you."

"I want my hundred bucks back," you say.

"I don't have it. I gave it to my wife."

"I'm sick of you and your French accent," you say. "Jump in and swim."

One-Arm rushes you, but you get a shot off. It hits him square in the chest, and he stumbles overboard.

"Christ," Trevor says.

"All right, Jean, move it," you say.

He walks to the stern and pauses for a second, like he is thinking of a worthy last line. The wind is flapping his trousers and even his normally slick hair is blowing around.

"You are making a mistake," he says. "I pray for your souls."

With Jean overboard, you stand on the bow watching until he is a couple hundred yards away. In the cold water, he'll never make it back. Pulling away you see him struggling back toward his boat, but sinking with every stroke.

———————◆•◆•◆———————

Jean and the other men you killed are far behind you when the clouds open up. You steer closer to land. The two of you take turns studying the shore through the rain and spray.

"Jesus," Trevor moans.

You nod. Caught in the waves, your boat is a giant's plaything. Once, she nearly rolls. You have the barrels too far on the starboard side.

"Better move 'em," you say over the wind. "Take the wheel."

Working with the post-digger, you move the barrels, one by one, inside the net, to the middle of the stern. Now the load is centered.

"Much better," you say, back at the wheel.

Trevor drinks from his flask in big gulps, like he has a thirst he can never quench. His mouth slightly open, he stares in the direction of land.

"We ain't making it, are we?"

"We will."

You say to yourself that you are a clever, handy man and that you will figure out a way to get the two of you back safely. You tell the Spirit that if he will just see you through this, you will give up your bootlegging, your womanizing, your gambling, your schemes, your drinking. You promise the Spirit this while the sea shakes your boat.

Trevor continues to drink. Hail spews down and breaks one of the windows. You squint at the shore for a cove, some kind of safe inlet where you can ride out the storm, but there's nothing but jagged cliffs as far as you can see. And then you spy a cutter, a distant black speck, headed towards you.

"Cutter," you say. "Let's get 'em overboard."

Trevor is very drunk now, leaning against the cabin with his legs spread wide and the hail pelting his face.

"Why don't we just cut them loose?"

You shake him. "What the hell is wrong with you, Trevor? Now let's go!"

You unload. The cutter looms on the far waves, crashing and slicing through the dense water. By the time the barrels are all dumped, the cutter is only a hundred yards away, and a voice from a loudspeaker shouts through the storm.

"Ahoy! Are you okay?"

You flash your lights to signal OK. You don't know much Morse Code, but you know enough to signal OK.

"Get your vessel to port immediately," the voice says. You signal OK again.

The cutter circles your boat and tears back out to sea.

"Let's bring 'em in again," you say.

With a gaff on the end of a long pole, Trevor hooks the cable at the stern. You connect the cable to the winch and hit the switch. Nothing happens. You feel a rush of heat beneath your sweater. You try the switch again. Nothing. Sweat clings to your upper lip. You lick it off.

"Told you that winch wouldn't last," Trevor says.

"Shit." It's all you can say.

The boat rolls impotently over the swells, and the drag from the net full of barrels sticks the boat in the water like the mud did your logging truck in the forest. Waves pounding on the port side surge you toward shallow water, near the cliffs.

"Cut 'em loose," Trevor says frantically.

"No."

"We can't do anything," he says. "We gotta."

When you aren't looking, Trevor gets an axe and scrambles toward the stern with it. You grab his arm and nail him in the jaw with your fist. He falls to the deck with a mighty slap, like a freshly caught tuna. Back at the wheel, you power up the boat.

"Come on, Lizzie," you say.

The engine roars, you smell the heavy exhaust, and the boat crawls forward. But the waves are relentless hammers against the port side, and just as you get the bow facing the waves, your feet vibrate and there is an unmistakable crunch. Looking out the rear doorway, you see the water, bubbling out of the engine hatch. The motor is snuffed out.

Stepping out onto the deck, you open your own pint of whiskey, take a deep drink. You shake Trevor. He comes to, rubbing his jaw. He looks at you and knows you are both screwed.

"We can still swim," you shout.

You yank off your bulky slicker and boots. The shore is only half a mile away at most. Might make it if the cold doesn't get you. The whiskey warmed you. You might make it.

"Hey, Trevor," you say. "Look."

At the top of a promontory, a light shines. A house, maybe a couple. Whatever it is, it's something to swim for.

"Should have known this is how we'd end up," Trevor says.

You drink the rest of the whiskey and toss the flask to the sharks. Plunging in, you scrabble a few yards in the icy water before you notice Trevor, still shivering on the deck. You yell at him to join you, but the waves smother your voice and you have all you can do to get to the surface and breathe. Then, in a lull between the waves, you start swimming. After a while, the cold is strangely refreshing. You can still taste the warm whiskey in your throat. Not so bad.

You were a clever, handy man, you tell yourself.

Seven Whole Grains on a Mission™

The following text was transcribed from a digital audio recorder found by a goat herdsman high in the mountains of Afghanistan. It is the last account of a man who was indeed the epitome of his company's tagline: Seven whole grains on a mission™.

8 August– [*sound of throat clearing*]...Arrived, Kabul, 6:15 p.m. local time. Now in my room at the Kabul Serena, having survived the usual harrowing flight.

The airplane graveyard on the fringes of the airport has doubled in size since I was last here. Hardly inspires confidence. Neither do the customs officers with their disturbingly hirsute mustaches. The heaps of rubbish and rubble, the dust, the women in those mesh-faced *burqas*...[*sigh*]...nothing changes here.

In case I should lose this recorder, my undercover name is John Smith and my permanent address is Corus Hotel Hyde Park, 1-7 Lancaster Gate, London W2 3LG, ENGLAND. For identification purposes I stand 6 feet tall and weigh 13 stone or 182 pounds exactly. Furthermore, I have excellent teeth for an Englishman; I floss daily and have never smoked.

I work for Kashi, an innovative cereal company based in the States. La Jolla, California, to be precise. You've seen their adverts on the tele—some handsome American devil trekking about the globe in a safari jacket, searching for new grains to add to their already popular and salubrious seven-grain mix (hard red winter wheat, long-grain brown rice, barley, oats, rye, buckwheat and triticale).

The adverts are true. Kashi really does hire adventurous sorts to ferret out new grain possibilities. But they're not Americans. Everyone seems to hate them at the moment. They're Aussies or Brits, like myself. All told, there are seven of us Global Grain Explorers.

I am GGE7. This is my report.

9 August– [*sound of a sliding door*]…It's…let's see… half-past two in the morning. Standing on the balcony. In the daylight, I have a lovely view of Zarnegar Park, but at the moment it's pitch black out there and I can only hear the splashing of the fountain in the courtyard. This section of the city is truly an oasis of luxury amidst absolute squalor. The hotel is also close to both the embassy and the airport, should events take a turn and I need to dash.

Other impressions. Ah, yes. The guide and interpreter Kashi hired for this mission seems a pleasant enough fellow. His name is Fahim. Had a nice chin-wag with him when he arrived at the hotel last night. I offered to get him a room, but he wouldn't hear of it. Instead he curled up beneath my desk, a habit he acquired during the somewhat haphazard American bombing campaign following 9/11. Dreadful business. The bombing, that is. Not his sleeping sweetly beneath my desk. Threw an afghan on top of him—excuse me, I mean the blanket, not a local or the shaggy hound. Anyway, after washing down a box of TLC Blackberry Graham Soft-Baked Cereal Bars with a couple of single malts, I studied my briefing documents.

The truth is, I'm rather annoyed at being sent here on what amounts to an investigation into my predecessor's disappearance. He was last seen in the hotel's business centre, emailing GGE HQ. It was the final communication they received from him. It reads:

[*sound of paper unfolding*]

> To the Watch Officer:
> In a few minutes, I shall embark on my quest for the elusive spillit grain, but I first wanted to report some dodgy goings-on since arriving at the Kabul Serena.
> First, on my way to breakfast this morning, I tripped on some bloke sleeping in front of my door. When I shouted to him, he ran away snickering. Quite sure the bugger nicked my newspaper.
> Then, while packing the Land Rover, Rasheed discovered a flat tyre. It had been slashed. Fortunately, we had a spare.
> Finally, when I complained about my missing newspaper, the manager smiled queerly at me and said, 'Goodbye, sir'. The way he said it—like a James Bond villain—was quite unsettling, and I was fortunate to have a GOLEAN Malted Chocolate Crisp chewy bar in my pocket. I sat on the terrace and enjoyed the bar with some of the strong coffee they fancy here, and pondered the situation.
> Despite these bizarre events, I am undaunted in my task. Stories of the Afghani spillit grain and its

incredible antioxidant properties, while considered apocryphal by the Western agricultural establishment, are too rich with nutritional promise to ignore. I must go after it.

As I note in my Grain Exploration Proposal, spillit is thought to explain why the hermit tribesmen of the Hindu Kush mountain range have an average life expectancy of 113 years. In any event, according to the goat herders familiar with this territory, the spillit grows on the steppes of the Hindu Kush, and I intend to find it.

Wish me well. I shall return in one month's time.
Cheers,
GGE6

[*sound of paper refolding*]

Not sure what I'm getting into here. My predecessor may have gotten lost, been kidnapped, or—God forbid—gone native. We all know what happened to Kurtz in *Heart of Darkness*, not to mention that Marlow chap that went to find him. Perhaps I'll find him ensconced in a cave high in the mountains. Who knows? Need to get some sleep. Fahim is sleeping soundly, so why can't I?

10 August– Been a long day. Departed the hotel at dawn and set out on the Salang Road north. Encountered four checkpoints. At one, some bored American soldiers were attempting to engage in one of the local pastimes— goat fighting—but the goats were thirsty and listless and having none of it. Was glad for the dozen cases of Kashi cereals we brought as bribes. Gave each checkpoint a box of Flakes and Honey Puffs. One checkpoint asked if we had cold milk. Cheeky bastards.

We've made camp on the roadside tonight. Lamb kabobs and rice for dinner. It's getting cold, so I think I'll turn in now.

[*Hours of snoring and sleep-talking were not transcribed.*]

11 August– Arrived at our jumping-off point: the base of the Hindu Kush range. Overjoyed to be here. A lorry stalled in front of us in the Salang Tunnel, and Fahim and I nearly suffocated from the fumes. The road was terribly narrow, with no guardrails. Bloody awful day.

Tomorrow we begin our climb into the highlands to find the elusive spillit grain. Fahim spoke with the pack train handlers and promised them each two boxes of Kashi⸱ Heart to Heart™ Oat Flakes & Wild Blueberry Clusters. Wish he'd checked with me first. We haven't enough of the Oat Flakes & Wild Blueberry Clusters. Shall have to substitute some Nuggets or GOLEAN Crunch!™ Honey Almond Flax. Both have high nutritional value and excellent flavour.

Note to self: must requisition new recorder. This one appears to be malfunctioning.

15 August– Altitude adjustment. Bloody torture is what it is, every time. Haven't had the strength at the end of the day to continue my report.

Finally made it to base camp. Will settle here for a few days to acclimatize to the thin air, then we're continuing up to the steppes, where I'm confident we'll find the spillit. If it's there, it should be about harvest time.

19 August– Were about to embark yesterday when a goat herder came by and Fahim foolishly agreed to fight one of his animals. Bets were taken, the goat given 3:1 odds against Fahim. The lad was doing an admirable job fending off the cantankerous beast, then lost his footing and was gored in the leg. Didn't penetrate anything vital, thank God, but we shall have to wait a few days before continuing. I hope nothing happens to him because our pack handlers don't speak a lick of English, and I can't understand a syllable of Pashto or Dari.

Kashi˙ really needs to improve its employee language training programmes—for the GGE's especially.

24 August– Tragedy struck today. A rock tumbling down the hillside spooked one of the pack mules. The mule turned to run, tangling up the lines, then lost its footing and fell over the cliff, taking half the string and three of our handlers with it. I shall never forget their milk-curdling screams. They took better than half our supplies, and almost all of the Kashi˙, with them. Most unnerving. Tomorrow we—

[*sound of tent flaps rustling*]

"Yes, Fahim?"

"The handlers are fearful, Mr. Smith. They say this trip is cursed. No Westerner has ever tasted the spillit grain, and is not supposed to. They believe it is a sign from Allah."

"Bloody Allah, my arse, Fahim. They knew our mission before we left. What do they want?"

"More money."

"Of course. How much?"

"Ten thousand pounds."

"Not dollars?"

"No. They said the dollar has been losing against the Euro and the Pound, so they want pounds sterling."

[*sigh*]

"Very well. But only once we return, and *only* if we are successful."

"We will be, Mr. Smith."

[*sound of tent flaps rustling; recorder switched off*]

25 August– Travel is brutally slow now. Water, scarce. Nothing but rocks and dust in this region. Can't wait until we reach those lush high plains.

Had another scare. While wending up a precipitous trail, we saw some activity in the valley below. Took cover and produced my binoculars for a better look. At least a dozen men in white robes kneeled on a rug facing East, AK-47s within arm's reach. Fahim thinks they were Taliban.

Everyone in the Hindu Kush seems to have a gun. Beginning to regret our leaving without one. Will have to travel more by night to avoid detection.

27 August– Stumbled into an American patrol yesterday. Nearly got ourselves shot. I was brought to an American lieutenant for questioning. Told him I was a GGE with Kashi. He thought my badge was a fake, but believed me once he found the cereal. Said I shouldn't be wandering in this territory without a weapon. In exchange for most of our remaining cereal, he gave me a spare M4A1 carbine with a grenade launcher. The cereal is as good as gold in these barren parts.

Before I left, I made the mistake of mentioning we'd spotted Taliban. The lieutenant eyed me for a moment, shrugged, then reached deep into a box of Organic Promise® Cinnamon Harvest. He took a fistful of those organic wheat biscuits with a fusion of warm, spicy organic cinnamon and organic evaporated cane juice crystals and shoved them in his mouth. Crumbs covered his shirt. He wiped his face with the back of his hand and asked me what I was doing here.

I'd already explained myself, but I went through it again: that I worked for Kashi, that I was on a mission to find the elusive spillit grain, and that, according to my sources, it was being cultivated on the nearby steppes. The lieutenant said that one of his patrols had passed some fields about 20 klicks to the northeast. When he attempted to tell me what that distance was in kilometers, I interrupted him.

"I know. It's twenty kilometers or twelve-point-four miles. I was British SAS, young man."

I shan't forget his most American reply: "Well, *lah-dee-dah*." His cheeks were chipmunk-full with Cinnamon Harvest. I wished he bloody choked.

28 August– Lost another pack handler today. After lunch he excused himself to use the latrine, and dashed. Took a mule and one of our last skeins of water with him, the bugger. If I see him again, I'm going to test out the M4A1 grenade launcher on him.

29 August– At daybreak, we came over a ridgeline and spied one of the most beautiful vistas I have ever seen: a vast field of ripe spillit waving in the early morning breeze. The dew glistened in the pink sunlight.

Unfortunately, the field was occupied by at least 100 women harvesting the grain with scythes, while 20 men with AK-47s guarded the perimeter. Fahim has offered to go down alone and ask to buy some of the grain from them. It may be our best option. I haven't ammunition enough to mow down the guards.

By far, this has been my riskiest Grain Expedition yet. Once, in the jungles of Borneo, some angry tribesmen threatened to roast me and my translator alive, but they were palliated by boxes of Mighty Bites. Actually, they ignored the cereal and amused themselves with the boxes themselves, which they cleverly fashioned into droll little hats. At the moment, however, I am entirely out of goodies with which to bribe. I shall have to improvise.

31 August– Fahim entered the field waving a white flag, spoke with a guard, and was summarily executed. My sole remaining pack handler immediately fled, and when the guards saw him, they shot him as well. The pickers scattered, leaving only the armed men in my sights.

At that moment, something barbarous rose up in me. I launched grenade after grenade at them. Their body parts were dashed across the field like exploded bits of the ripe real strawberries in our TLC soft-baked cereal bars. In minutes, all 20 of them were dead, and the lingering smoke smelled of toasted spillit grain.

With my gun at the ready, I ran down into the valley, grabbed one of the sacks of grain and retreated back to the ridge. Tears welled up in my eyes as I ran my fingers through the grain and inhaled its rich, ripe, woody scent. Much like barley. I strapped it to the last mule and headed out.

It is now dark. The mule and I are camped about five klicks away from the American soldiers. When I reach them tomorrow, I'll request an armed escort back to Kabul. Since I'm returning with the grain, I'm sure Kashi will be glad to reimburse the U.S. military for their trouble. Out of rations, so I am eating the spillit. Delicious, even raw.

1 September– Morning…horrible stomach cramps. Limbs trembling. Thirst…terrible. The mule has disappeared, along with the grain.

Can't understand what is happening. Unless…the spillit may need to be cooked first.

No!

Warning to Kashi! The spillit…it's…poi—

[*sounds of recorder dropping, wind over the microphone*]

THE BLONDE IMPERATIVE

From the moment he met Alice McCormick, his counterpart for the executive retreat, Shelby Fox felt himself caught in a reality distortion field that prevented his making rational decisions. Tall, aristocratically curvy, and with chatoyant blue eyes, Alice was a genetic jackpot.

His instant attraction to her posed two problems. First, she was a blonde, and every entanglement with them had led to disaster. Second, they were both married, and unlike some who treated these conferences as opportunities to play around, Shelby loathed situational ethics.

Her name was another issue. Besides blondes, over the years he'd gotten into mischief with Alices: shoplifting, drinking and driving, hitting on bisexual strippers, and hopping a southbound freight train in February and nearly freezing to death during the 50 mile ride. Since Alice the Speechwriter was both the quintessential blonde *and* an Alice, Shelby worried her effect on him might be doubled, making her another *Alice in Wonderland* capable of upending his entire universe.

When Shelby first learned that Alice would be writing for the Foods division CEO, he was mistakenly told her name was Constance, conjuring up an image of a sharp-jawed hellcat ten minutes out of Columbia journalism school, instead of the magnetic mid-30s goddess who sat beside him now in Ballroom B. Alice wore a cornflower silk blouse and a knee-length black pleated skirt. Crossing her trim legs, she studied her laptop screen and typed changes as her CEO rehearsed from the podium. She tilted her head towards the stage and tucked some hair behind her ear, a gesture that, combined with the breath of unfamiliar perfume it sent his way, he found poignantly sexy. Shelby's entire body was tense and faintly trembling, and he hadn't taken a deep breath since check-in at the Scottsdale resort when Alice shamelessly shook out her considerable hair. She had rolled her neck and dipped her head backwards as though rinsing her hair beneath an island waterfall. Shelby was agape. Like all things soft and pretty, that glistening curtain of gold cried out to be stroked.

Under the ballroom table, her shoe tapped his leg. When he snapped out of his reverie, she was smiling at him, scrunching her eyes into amused slits. She quickly typed something and an instant later a message appeared in his computer chat window:

"What's up with you? Why so spacey?"

"Nothing," he replied. *"Preoccupied, that's all."*

"Everything all right?"

Shelby was far from all right. At first he was going to reply with another banality, but expressing his feelings in text form emboldened him. After looking in her eyes and seeing only enticement there, he decided to announce how he really felt.

"It's you, you're making me crazy—CRAZY! I want to..."

He paused to consider his words, to find, as Flaubert would put it, *"Le mot juste."* He questioned the wisdom of expressing himself so directly, but to hell with it, he decided, you only live once.

"...I want to ravage you."

A second later this appeared on his screen:

"You want to *destroy* me? I believe you mean you want to *ravish* me."

She pasted the dictionary definition of "ravish" at the end of the message.

"You're right," he typed. *"See what you're doing to me? Yes, I want to RAVISH you."*

The CEO stopped his rapid-fire droning. "Alice?" He leaned over the podium. "Any thoughts so far?"

"Yes, Bob," she said. "You need to slow down. This is complex information you're asking the audience to absorb, and you've been rattling it off at"—she consulted a stopwatch on her phone—"almost a hundred and forty words per minute. To be effective, you really need to be down around one-ten, one-twenty."

"Well, how do you propose I do that?"

"By taking a small breath at the end of each sentence. Or by counting to three in your head. That's what periods are for, sir. Use them. You need to give time for each concept to sink in."

"I see."

"Why don't you start at the beginning?"

"Very good."

Alice spoke into a small walkie-talkie: "From the top, Jim. Thanks."

The CEO drank some water, stood tall and gazed at the TelePrompTer glass until the words began their upward crawl. He was noticeably slower this time.

"*Good advice,*" Shelby wrote.

"*Thanks, but the speech needs tweaking, and I do my best writing near water. Care to join me out at the pool after this for a little tanning and revising? Maybe we could trade speeches? How about it?*"

Shelby didn't do his best work near water, and certainly not in public like those writer-performance artists at Starbucks; he did his best work in a study carrel in the college library basement back home. But the prospect of literally seeing more of fair-haired Alice was too tempting to resist.

"*Sounds good.*"

This time when he pressed ENTER, his entire body tingled.

After rehearsals, as the two of them walked through the hotel with their laptop bags, Alice reached out and rubbed his suit fabric.

"Great drape on that suit, by the way. It flows on you."

"Thanks. I like your skirt. Old schoolgirl uniform?"

"I'll never tell," she said. "Half an hour then?"

"Okay."

"Let's get a cabana near the waterfall. We'll need some shade out there. I want to tan, not broil."

"Will do," he said.

"So...*Shelby.* Why would your parents give you such a name?"

"The Shelby Cobra."

"The what?"

"It's a sports car. My father loved it and thought the name sounded cool, so here I am."

"And your middle name is Cobra, I presume." She looked at him askance, biting her lower lip.

"Hmm…Alice McCormick. Any relation to the reaper?"

"I don't even know what a reaper does. You?"

"Yeah, it reaps," he said. "Wheat. Corn, too, I think."

Corn. Shelby and a blonde named Ellis were tramping across a Connecticut cornfield dragging Rollaboards. It was the day before Thanksgiving and the ground was stiff. For some reason the field hadn't been harvested yet, and the dried and yellowed stalks brushed their jackets and rustled in a raw wind. There were rooftops in the distance, a town where Shelby hoped there'd be a train station.

An hour earlier, he and the girl had been cosily ensconced on a Peter Pan bus to Hartford, after having eyed each other from opposite benches in South Station. Like Shelby, she was clearly a college student on her way home for the long weekend. They introduced themselves. Her name was Ellis, and she wore a Boston University baseball cap over a blonde bob. Her hair sliced across her cheek, swooping to a point towards her lips, which glistened with pink lip gloss. Once on the bus, he sat near the back, next to the window, and was about to close his eyes when she sat down beside him with a trenchcoat on her lap. She read a curled copy of Kant's *Grounding for the Metaphysics of Morals.* When he politely inquired about the book, she explained Kant's idea of a categorical imperative—*Act only according to that maxim whereby you can, at the same time, will that it should become a universal law*—segueing into the philosopher's related argument that one should never tell a lie. For reasons Shelby didn't fully grasp, even if a murderer were looking for somebody, one had to tell the truth about the person's whereabouts.

Suddenly glowering at him with the unwavering eyes of a gunslinger, she demanded to know if he thought she was pretty. Shelby said she was.

"Now, wasn't that freeing?" Ellis said. "Direct, always direct—that's how I roll. Now you? You're cute enough to make a girl quit studying for finals."

He chuckled and leaned back for a nap.

Somewhere on the Mass Pike, he awoke. The afternoon sun was on his face when he became aware of a pleasant thumping in his lap. His whole body felt warm. His buttocks were tensed, his pelvis elevated as though being hoisted by an invisible rope. He opened his eyes. Ellis's trenchcoat covered his lap, and one of her hands was moving up and down rhythmically underneath. With her free hand, she continued to read. Shelby's eyelids fluttered. Glancing over the seat back, he thought he saw the bus driver scowl at him, but the reservoir of well-being rising in him diverted his attention. Faster and faster the coat bounced in his lap, like a coked-up frog hopping frantically to get out. When he was close, and his breath shallowed, she gave him a salacious sidelong glance. The words "On a Supposed Right to Lie" came sharply into focus next to her puckering lips. After he spasmed in the seat, she placed Kant on her knee and slid her other hand underneath clutching a handkerchief.

A few miles beyond the Sturbridge toll booth, the bus made an unscheduled exit, pulling over beside a desolate cornfield. The brakes hissed. They were kicked off the bus and had to walk a gauntlet of snickering, heckling college students. Outside, a hot cloud of diesel fumes like volcanic ash engulfed them, and when it dissipated they were alone on an empty road in a raw wind.

Luggage in tow, they trudged across the cornfield only to be met on the other side by a police cruiser. When the officer asked why they had been kicked off the bus, Ellis, of course, told the truth, and the two of them spent the evening before Thanksgiving in a police station. And thus his long and sordid history with blondes began. When Ellis's parents picked her up, she waited until they had left the room before French-kissing him on her way out. "See you, Shelby," she said.

"See you soon, Shelby," Alice said.

The hotel room door banged shut behind him. In the bathroom, Shelby ran the tap and repeatedly splashed his hot cheeks, unable to cool them. Recalling the incident on the bus and being in palpably close proximity to Alice had made his brain sing. He soaked a hand towel in cold water, wrapped it around his neck and lay down on the bed.

It was the stress. The stress and the urgency. The need for constant rewrites with instant turnaround, right up until the moment the executive swaggered onstage to blaring music, flashing lights and a ballroom full of sycophants clapping and hooting like cultists at a Tony Robbins event. Chances are, if he'd met Alice in a less keyed-up setting, he wouldn't be going through the agony of temptation that he was now.

That was crap and he knew it. The fact was, the second he'd walked onboard the corporate jet with the CEO of the Beverages division, Stephen Sweet (no kidding), and he saw Alice dreamily swiveling in the cushy seat, staring at her computer monitor and wiggling her lips, Shelby knew he was in Trouble with a capital-T, and that rhymes with P, which stands for Pool—where he was headed in a few minutes.

How many times did his encounters with blondes have to end in scorched earth before he learned his lesson?

Maybe he could keep it light with Alice, keep it Platonic. After they worked on the speeches, they could play mini-golf, or hit the driving range. Shelby groaned. Sure, the driving range. The exact place he encountered Naomi, the blonde who inadvertently caused the break-up with his then-girlfriend, Jennifer.

He was at an IBM executive's house in Camden, Maine, sailing around the Fox Islands with him as the executive "thought out loud" for the speech Shelby was writing. On his day off, Shelby meandered north to a driving range in Bangor. There he spied Naomi, a blonde with hair that shone like wet straw drying in the sun, swiping at a golf ball and missing, nearly falling over with each effort. Of course, Shelby had to help her. He showed her the proper stance and was soon hugging her back with his front, unaware that a local TV news crew was there. The story that aired suggested they were a couple in love, a suggestion furthered by Naomi's laughing at Shelby's jokes, waving that yellow hair around and flashing her excellent teeth. His girlfriend's grandmother, from Portland, saw the piece and told Jennifer. He and Naomi had had dinner and made out, sure, but the worst part of the incident—besides the breakup with Jennifer—was that the footage showed him only slicing the ball. He'd made some awesome drives that day.

Now there was Alice to contend with. His very genes craved her, and even though he knew no good could come of this, even though he had formulated a categorical imperative of his own (*Stay the hell away from blondes*), and even though he was conflicted by guilt for considering being unfaithful to his wife, he was certain the Creator wouldn't have put Alice in his path just to tempt him. Meeting her, an intelligent and beautiful fellow speechwriter, seemed momentous. Pregnant with destiny.

He said a short prayer, telling the Creator "Thy will be done," but the truth was, he wanted a wink from the universe that said if he chose to shag Alice for the remainder of their stay, it was okay. "Amen," he said, but he felt no relief. In fact, he felt more confused now than before the prayer.

Groping over his shoulder, he pulled the Gideons from the bedside table drawer, opened to a random page, shucked the towel off his face, and read. The passage was from Ecclesiastes, and the sense it gave him of being watched made his throat cinch up:

> *And I find more bitter than death*
> *The woman whose heart is snares and nets,*
> *Whose hands are fetters.*
> *He who pleases God shall escape from her,*
> *But the sinner shall be trapped by her.*

Shelby sat up on the bed and took some deep breaths. Without thinking he reached for his cell phone and dialed his wife.

"Hey, *you*," she said. "Aren't you supposed to be working?"

"We're on a break."

"I have a surprise for you when you get home."

"What is it?"

"Like I'm going to tell you."

Shelby started to cry. He sniffed.

"What's wrong?" she asked.

For a flickering instant, he recalled Ellis's monologue about why one should never lie. *"Maybe,"* he thought to himself, *"but Kant was never married."*

"Nothing," he said. "It's the room. Allergies. The carpet, think."

"Well, I think there are pills in your toiletry bag. If not, the gift shop will probably have some. Better yet, go have yourself a spa treatment. Steve Sweet did say *anything* you want, right? You have *carte blanche*, so use it!"

"Maybe. I have to get back."

"Sweet of you to call. So spontaneous."

"Smoochy," he said.

"Smoochy. Bye."

Shelby hung up and looked around. The furniture, the walls, the light from the bathroom—everything was scrutinizing him, waiting to see what he did next. His breath was shallow and guilty.

Through the balcony window, the pool water glinted. It beckoned to him.

———◆———

It was the first time he'd ever lain in the sun in the Southwest, and it was a more intense heat than anything he'd ever experienced. The thermometer at the poolside bar read 103°F, but it was a dry heat. Dry? It was positively desiccating. Shelby drank some of his fruit smoothie and kept an eye on the entryway near the waterfall, where, any moment he hoped, Alice would appear.

Everything around him seemed divinely orchestrated to remind him of his many misadventures with blondes. He closed his eyes and the trickling waterfall across the courtyard took him back to spelunking with Laura, the curly-haired Cornell geologist, and then the heat on his skin reminded him of that sweltering August morning on Mount Washington, and how he almost fell into Tuckerman's Ravine because he had been admiring Laura's granite-hard rockhound's butt. The smell of tanning lotion awakened with startling clarity a memory of the summer he worked in Provincetown as a motel handyman. Shelby could see the motel maid, Adele—a British blonde bisexual—lying by the pool, smearing her arms with lotion, then the two of them making love in Shelby's cottage with the salt breeze wafting in, and finally, with a wince, the fistfight he had, and very nearly lost, with Adele's butch girlfriend from Liverpool. A few chaises down from Shelby, a man turned a page in his newspaper and Shelby was reminded of his editor firing him. Shelby had been sleeping with his editor's girlfriend, but he couldn't help himself. Tina, a blonde radio drive-time DJ, had a voice that was sheer liquid sex, the moonshine of women's voices—a distilled reincarnation of Marilyn Monroe's. Everything Tina said—from "Hiya, Shelby" to "There's a fender-bender on Route 9, folks" to "Gimme an Alabama Slammer"—she said as though she were at a bedroom door in black lace lingerie, coaxing Shelby inside. Her vocal chords were mysteriously tuned to the exact frequency of his genitals, and he had many opportunities to listen to Tina's voice—particularly at the upper registers—in a variety of beds, culminating in her boyfriend's, which turned out to be Shelby's editor's bed. Unfortunately, Shelby had been recording her voice and their lovemaking sessions for posterity, and forgot his briefcase by the bedside. The hot flush of embarrassment Shelby felt when his editor played the tape was even hotter than he felt now, sizzling in the Arizona glare.

He sprang up in his chaise, shielding his eyes, and scanned the poolside. No sign of Alice. Seeing the cabana tent still empty, Shelby swam a quick backstroke lap, toweled off and bought two giant frozen margaritas with salt. He put on his shirt and lay down in the shade of the cabana. He opened his laptop and spread out a draft of the speech so it looked as if he'd been working. He sipped the margarita. What if she'd already been out here, gotten bored and left? Between daydreaming, calling his wife and getting spooked by Scripture, he'd taken longer than expected to get out here. For all he knew, Alice was inside seething and would ignore him for the rest of the event.

He happened to be gazing at the waterfall when in his blurred periphery he saw her. At first all that registered was a tall shape with a lot of bare skin. Then his eyes focused on her. She wore a Tiffany blue bikini with white trim. Chin up and shoulders back, her blonde hair made bouffant by a white plastic hair band, Alice looked like a *Price Is Right* model showcasing a grand prize trip to Bali.

God, you shouldn't have made this woman so beautiful. Why tempt me like this? Screw you, it's not fair.

She smiled at him and scrunched her shoulders as she passed the lifeguard stand. Stepping under the cabana awning, she plopped a canvas tote on the chaise opposite and reached for a margarita.

"Oh, I love you." She took a sip, closing her eyes and licking her lips. "You have no idea how much I've wanted one of these. You've been working, I see. Get any sun?"

She sat down and studied him. Her legs were crossed and a white Dr. Scholl's sandal dangled from her foot. Shelby hadn't noticed the prosaic footwear earlier, for obvious reasons.

"Oh, sure," she said, the margarita poised in front of her, "you got some color. I must look like snow, don't I?"

He was about to take her question as an invitation to ogle every last inch of her, but he locked eyes with her instead.

"No, you look perfectly healthy," he said.

"Oh? Is that your considered professional opinion?"

"As a matter of fact, yes." He swung his feet onto the cement and faced her with his elbows on his knees. "You meet all the criteria for a great speech. A-I-D-A. Attention, Interest, Desire, and Action."

"I believe that's *Decision* and Action," she said.

"Whatever. That too."

She giggled. Then her face became serious and her breath deepened. Shelby's vision narrowed until there were only her eyes. The noises of the pool—a waitress taking a drink order, water lapping on the steps, the clang of a metal gate somewhere—hushed as though he and

Alice were descending together in a bathysphere. As they stared into each other's eyes, Shelby felt an electrical arc building between them and knew that any moment it would overwhelm him, prodding him to pounce on her right there in the cabana. Alice looked away and blushed.

"I...I need a minute." She got up and walked around the pool sipping her drink. A group of executives watched her. When she returned, she sat down on the chaise and opened her computer without looking at him.

"We should probably get started," she said.

"Yeah."

"Let me proof mine one more time, then let's trade, okay?"

"Sure."

Alice went immediately to work, scrolling through her text while sipping the margarita. She even managed to get a waiter's attention to order two more. How was she was so easily able to block out what had just transpired between them? Shelby tried to read his own speech but kept losing focus by the second page. Finally, he clapped his computer shut.

"Alice, what are we going to do?"

"About?" Her typing slowed.

"This," he said. "Us."

She stopped typing, sighed and gazed at a row of palm trees across the pool. "I *don't* know." She grabbed her margarita and took a sip. The red of her lips, Shelby noticed, matched her fingernails and toes. Shaking her head, she put down the drink and started typing again, pounding the keys with impunity. "You know what I can't wait for?"

"What?"

She banged rapid-fire on the DELETE key.

"The day I don't have to shoehorn the *non-word* 'synergy' into a speech thirty-seven times," she said. "One of these days an exec is going to bring that word up and I'm going to say, 'You know what? Fuck synergy and fuck you. I'm not writing it. Oh, what's that? I'm fired? Fine, I'll just go write for the Ambassador to France.'" She winked at him. "I'm fluent in French, you know."

"Really?"

"Absolument, parlé et écrit."

The waiter brought the drinks. She polished off her first one and slapped it on his tray, signing the bill and chirping to the waiter, *"Vous êtes homme adorable et jeune."*

The waiter smiled. Shelby took in Alice's aphrodisiacal figure stretched out on the chaise, beginning with her toenails, which red he would name "Hot Kiss in a Cold Rain" if he were naming nail polishes, all the way to her ears.

Suddenly he felt his age, and not because of the slight padding on his once Grecian abs or the twinge in his lower back from so many years of planting butt to chair for a living, but because he realized he was, with a blonde no less, on the precipice of an *affair*—an artificial-sounding word that he had only ever heard in movies. As a boy, his current age had seemed a lifetime away, but it wasn't anymore. That time—a time he had once imagined would include flying cars and space travel—was now. Realizing this filled him with a craving for youth that gnawed at his entire being from behind his navel, and it was in that moment that Shelby Fox understood why men and women had affairs. It wasn't out of love or even lust; it was from a terrible, impossible desire to be young again, when everything is fresh and ahead of you.

A group of executives in golf attire strolled past their cabana, one of them nudging Alice's CEO. His eyes widened. He gave her a thumbs-up.

"Looking good, Alice."

She raised her drink. "Feeling good, Bob."

Shelby smiled and shook his head in awe. A *Trading Places* reference. One of his favorite movies. Cursed with blondes or not, he didn't care. Alice was a living dream, and he had to have her.

———◆·◆·◆———

As usual for these events, following the opening night banquet that evening there was some high-priced celebrity entertainment: a smoky-voiced pianist who specialized in the standards. When her first number opened with the line "There may be trouble ahead," Shelby and Alice looked at each other across the ballroom. He glanced at the door to the patio.

It was difficult to extricate themselves because they were at their respective CEO's tables, and the tables were an arm's length from the stage. Alice managed first, waiting until the performer launched into a piano solo, then slipping out the patio door. When the audience applauded at the end of the solo, Shelby gestured to Steve Sweet that he had to make a call.

Out on the patio, he looked for her in the terraced cactus garden. Everything was cloaked in shadows. The brick radiated heat. Shelby strode down a path that serpentined through the garden, quickening his steps at each turn because she wasn't there, until he rounded the final corner and was spilled out into a courtyard of sand. A fire flickered in a pit at the center, and he saw the outline of her gown with the plunging back. She sat on a stone bench facing the fire. Her hair was up, and the sides shimmered in the firelight.

He could feel sand getting in his shoes as he approached the fire. Alice's eyes glistened.

"You okay?" he asked.

She smiled and patted the stone bench. "I was just thinking about my father."

Mention of her father made Shelby uncomfortable. His shoulders tensed.

"The fireplace was going that night." She nodded at the fire pit, which popped and flew sparks. "That's why I thought of it. My mother was out at a bar when he collapsed. I called the ambulance and held him in my arms in front of that fire. He never said a word. He just went to sleep."

Shelby handed her his pocket square, silently congratulating himself for the chivalrous gesture. She dried her eyes. Having nothing equally tragic to share, he was unsure what to say, so he just held her. She shivered. He draped his suit jacket over her shoulders.

"Anyway, fireplaces do that to me," she said.

"Understandable."

Her hand glided around his back like silk on silk, and then her fingers were playing with the hair on his shirt collar. The look they gave each other was one of anticipation and fear. Alice traced his lips with the back of a fingernail.

"Room ten-eleven." She stood. "But please don't let anybody see you. We both have reputations to maintain. Give me fifteen minutes."

She spun around and wobbled across the sand, fading into the darkness until his last sight of her was her bare back gleaming in the firelight.

Inside, the lobby was empty. He wandered into the lounge and ordered a shot of Macallan 12-year. The bartender stood by with the bottle like a man with a fire extinguisher. Shelby sipped his second drink and stared at two distinguished older couples laughing across the bar. One of the wives, gloriously silver-haired, smiled at him. Her profile bore a jolting resemblance to his wife's. Shelby raised his glass to her, then, as soon as she turned away, he raised his eyes incredulously to the ceiling. When he finished the drink, he rapped the glass down, signed the bill and walked out wondering why they called it "liquid courage." He felt less courageous now than he had that afternoon. Right now, that faint trembling throughout his body was back, and he couldn't get enough breath in his lungs.

Alice didn't want anybody seeing him, so he decided to take a circuitous route to her room. From the lobby, he rode the elevator to the top floor and started down the long corridor. He considered turning back, calling her room and calling it off, but the pull from behind his navel was too strong.

The corridor was thickly carpeted, muffling his footsteps. The only noise was the gentle whisk of his suit. He was moving towards a line that was dangerous to cross.

But that line was either invisible or he hadn't crossed it yet, although stepping on the second elevator and punching the "1" button gave him a moment's pause. A small TV in the elevator wall played 15-second commercials, the next one inviting him to "Ski Vail!"

Been there, done that. He'd been a ski bum for three years, breezing down the slopes by day and bartending by night. He'd clinked beer cans with Clint and been asked by Schwarzenegger, "Do you mind if I smoke my *cigar* in your *bar?*" He'd also fallen hard for a blonde, an 18-year-old waitress named Theda who beamed and kissed him every time he came in for coffee and pie. And the anticipation he felt walking into her cafe and stomping the snow off his boots was exactly like the tugging sensation that now pulled him off the elevator and brought him to the door of 1011. He knocked.

Later on, he couldn't remember the door opening or his stepping into the room; all he could recall was that blonde hair, now unfurled, against that black gown and his announcing, "I have to kiss you." He backed her into the bathroom doorjamb at the same time that she cupped his cheeks. Their lips met softly at first, nibbling until they both lost control and began chomping at each other, tongues dueling, teeth colliding. Opening one eye during the kiss, he lifted her hair with the back of his hand and marveled with a muffled whimper at how smoothly it sluiced over his skin, like water over marble. Alice's lissome arms dangled around his neck, and despite her height, she felt fragile against him. *And deceptively light,* he thought, as he heaved her off the ground, carried her to the sofa and compressed her to the cushions with his body. *"Oh mon, Monsieur Fox."* She let out soft noises of release: a woman savoring expensive chocolate, or the sounds Theda had made when he rubbed her feet after a long shift at the cafe. They, too, had kissed like this, like the nuclear missiles were on their way. They might even have been in love. But the disaster came as inevitably with her as it did with every other blonde. When her ex-boyfriend learned that Shelby was growing pot in his apartment, he told the police. Shelby was arrested. And his lawyer's only counsel after posting bail? *Get in your car tonight and never come back to this state.*

Alice kissed his neck.

"Just a second," she said, sitting up. She took hold of her dress straps and dragged them off her shoulders, then dismantled his tie. She eased back into the sofa, her hair fanning out resplendently on the sage fabric. Shelby unzipped her dress and peeled it off, and at the very moment she lay before him, a mile of uncharted flesh in a black strapless bra, he thought of the adulterer in that story of Chekhov's, his favorite one, the one with the little dog. *Come to think of it, the lady that drives him to distraction in the story is also a blonde.* For the first time in his life, Shelby understood the end of that story both intellectually and now viscerally: "...the hardest and most difficult part was only beginning." This encounter with Alice would lead to more at other conferences, which would lead to their craving each other, which would lead to motel rendezvous in cities halfway, which would lead to some unforeseen downfall, sudden and swift, and this time, overwhelmed by the accumulation of so many regrets, he would have to kill himself, probably by pills while out of town. Shelby's hands froze on her smooth, parted thighs.

"We shouldn't," he said.

She stared at him, then the ceiling, without moving. "You're right," she said.

He stood up in a daze and swiped his suit jacket off the bed. A newspaper crossword puzzle was there.

"Crossword?" he said.

"Yeah." She worked the dress back over her shoulders. "Such as it is. Phoenix paper. It's no *Times*, that's for sure."

He slipped his jacket on and turned so he couldn't see her. "Alice, we have to stay away from each other."

"I know."

"This event and every one after that," he said. "How do we do it?"

In the reflection from the sliding glass door, he watched her grab a hairband and wrangle her hair into a ponytail.

"I'll take the West Coast, you take the East," she offered.

"Dividing line?"

"The Mississippi?"

"Who gets Chicago?" he asked.

"That's east. You do."

"Okay. And while we're here, you can have the pool. I want the lounge and the golf course, all right?"

"That's more than fair," she said.

He started for the door.

"Shelby?"

He didn't turn around.

"Yeah?"

"We'll always have Paris."

He nodded with a bitter smile, then snapped the door open. He was 20 feet down the hall before it clicked shut behind him.

Three days later, riding the airport escalator down to the street, he felt a tap on his shoulder.

"Surprise," the woman said. "I told you I had a surprise for you!"

It was his wife. Except that her hair, once light golden brown, was now a dirty blonde.

THE DOGCATCHER

It was one of those mid-October afternoons in the Hudson Valley when the foliage is so brilliant it hurts your eyes. I wore Armani sunglasses, and with the snap in the air, my Orvis leather flight jacket. Back in my closet, I had a great suit—a Hickey Freeman that cost me two grand—but in this business, first impressions are everything and the worn leather jacket says you'll *stick*.

In my pocket I had the flyer for the lost Rhodesian ridgeback. "SUBSTANTIAL REWARD," it advertised. Well, I'd learned the hard way to clarify an owner's idea of "substantial," and when I called this owner and heard the number, my testes withdrew from the shock. This reward made my previous ones look like skee ball tickets. I was flossed and freshly shaven and brimming with confidence. Despite the recent lull in my business, I was still the best damn dogcatcher around, and I was about to meet my first billionaire.

She lived in Wellington—that's Upstate, in horse country. My bread-and-butter work kept me close to New York City—Westchester, Connecticut, Long Island and Jersey. With the houses so close together and the tiny yards, there's less open space for missing dogs to roam, and no woods where the toys become snacks for roving coyotes. Wellington, on the other hand, was nothing but open space. Green hills rolled endlessly in every direction and horses grazed along explosively colorful tree lines.

Gillian Barnes, widow of the late Texas tycoon Roy Barnes, lived at the top of one of these hills. I'd done some quick research on the New York Social Diary website, studied a few photos of her and ascertained that Mrs. Barnes was a foxy 30-something equestrienne with a pert ass you could sharpen knives on. Apparently the woman enjoyed widowhood because at every event she had a different piece of arm-candy. Over the years I'd had opportunities to get a little *sumpthin* from satisfied or lonely female clients, but I almost never took the bait. Didn't want to dilute my value proposition. But for this long-legged, golden-haired damsel, I might make an exception.

The gate was open when I arrived. A red clay driveway snaked up and around the hill, and the house, a sprawling stone English manor, stood ominously at the top like one of those castles you see in cartoons. I passed fenced-in horse fields and stands of maple and oak, and finally parked my aging Jeep between a red Mercedes convertible and a silver Range Rover.

Hunter, my faithful beagle, was curled up on the passenger seat. I cracked the windows and left a Milk-Bone and water for him on the floor. There was no way of knowing how long this would take. Sometimes they wanted to get you out the door and looking for the dog immediately, sometimes they needed to cry on your shoulder for an hour. I hoped this would be a short one. I grabbed my vet bag and got out.

A Chinese lady with a limp opened the door. She frowned at my leather jacket and led me into a massive room with vaulted ceilings and windows that looked out on the Catskills to the west. Mrs. Barnes sat in a club chair in front of a fireplace big enough to roast a steer. Her golden hair streamed down the seat back. There was a chill outside, but nothing to merit the skin-melting inferno in this fireplace. She tilted a highball at the matching club chair across from her. I sat down.

"So, *you're* the dogcatcher," she said.

"I am."

"Would you care for a drink?"

"I'd love one—after I've found your dog."

"All business. I like that." She smirked at my veterinarian bag. "Is that your little toolkit?"

"Yes."

"Can I see your tools?"

"Maybe later," I said.

She sipped her drink. After studying me for a moment, she went to the fireplace, bent over and jabbed the logs with a brass poker. The beauty of that woman's glutes defied all laws of mathematical probability. Turning around she caught me leering and smiled at me through a curtain of hair. She sat down again and crossed her legs, gesturing at me with the highball glass.

"Tell me," she said, "do you always dress this well to meet with clients?"

"I'll be looking for your dog the second I leave here, so there's no time for appearances."

"Have you always been a dogcatcher?"

"I taught college for a while. Film studies."

"And you were…"

"Laid off. Master's degree, no Ph.D." I took out my notebook. "So, how long has your dog been missing, Mrs. Barnes?"

"Two days."

"And the dog's name is Kebo?"

"Yes."

"And when did you first notice him missing?"

"Yesterday morning. When I came down to breakfast, May Lee—the woman that let you in—she told me she'd searched the house and couldn't find Kebo. I organized a search of the grounds. The stables, the fields, the woods, the neighbors' properties—we looked everywhere."

"What did you find?"

"Only this." She reached down on the floor beside her chair and pulled up a large Ziploc bag with a liquor bottle inside. "It's some liquor called Calvados. I've never heard of it."

I had. *CAL*vados—or, as I knew it, the Devil's fruit juice.

"It's a fruit brandy, made usually from apples or pears. Very popular among the troops when we liberated Normandy during WWII."

"A little history lesson," she said. "How nice. Well, I thought it might be useful for prints."

For some reason, clients always thought I had access to the FBI crime lab. I don't know why. I'm a *dogcatcher*, for crissake.

"Maybe," I said. "But you're sure it doesn't belong to somebody that works here?"

"Positive."

"I'll take it with me. Is the mansion alarmed, Mrs. Barnes?"

"It is."

"And the people who have the code—you trust them?"

"Only May Lee and I have it, so yes, I do," she said.

"The dog was definitely in for the night?"

"Yes, it was cold that night. He sat here with me, in front of the fire."

"Very good," I said.

"How is that good?"

"It sets up a solid conditional."

"Huh?" she said.

"If we know the dog was in for the night, only one of two things could have happened. Either you or May Lee let him out, or somebody else broke in, reset the alarm, and took him."

"Somebody else? Who?"

"Not sure," I said. "What about a boyfriend? Did you give the code to one?"

"No. I'm not in a relationship right now."

I didn't mention the two dozen young men I'd seen her with on the New York Social Diary website. Apparently they were just escorts.

"Do you have any enemies?" I asked.

"Sort of. One ex-lover, but he never knew the code, and he's an idiot. He couldn't have pulled this off."

"What about your late husband?" I asked.

"Somebody who'd kidnap my *dog*? No."

I put the notebook away, took out my iPhone and plugged a microphone into it.

"Now, I'd like you to speak into this. Pretend you're calling for Kebo. Go ahead."

She furrowed her brow, shrugged, and called to the dog several times. I recorded it, and when I pressed STOP, a single tear rolled down her cheek.

"Please excuse me." She stood up and gave me the Ziploc bag with the bottle inside.

"While you're up," I said, "I'll need a few things. A recent photo of Kebo, a swatch of fabric from his bed, his favorite toy, and some of his wet food and snacks if he gets any. And I need a cash retainer. Two grand. That's to cover my expenses while I look for Kebo."

"I can do everything but the wet food. He gets filet mignon."

"That's fine, bring it," I said.

She squinted at me and walked away. I craned my neck around the seat back to admire the sleekness of her legs in the khaki breeches and the knee-high riding boots.

While she was out, I put another log on the fire and looked at photographs on the mantle: her late husband—a fat SOB—and several celebrities I recognized from the movies. Mrs. Barnes returned with a canvas tote and handed it to me. There were no signs she'd been crying. She'd even freshened her makeup.

"What will you do with the fabric?" she asked.

"I need Kebo's scent. The best tool I know of for finding dogs is another dog."

"Ah." She walked me to the door and gave me the world's most erotic handshake. "Good luck."

"I'll be in touch as soon as I have a lead," I said.

After a final up-and-down appraisal of me, she sashayed up the stairs, giving me an excellent view of those billion-dollar buttocks. On the landing she paused and spoke over her shoulder.

"Find Kebo quickly, and there will be a nice *bonus* for you."

Once I coiled up my tongue, I went outside for some cool air. I got Hunter out of the Jeep, let him take a good whiff of the swatch from Kebo's bed, and tagged along as he sniffed around the mansion. He picked up a scent from one of the service entrances in back, and he trotted down the clay driveway all the way to the gate. In the gate turnout next to the road, Hunter sniffed in circles and finally stopped. There were tire tracks, all right, and a dog's faded paw prints. I tossed Hunter a Milk-Bone.

"Good work, boy. Good work."

———◆———

I knew it was pointless before I even started, but I had a process that had always worked for me, and my rule of thumb was, in the absence of strong clues to follow, follow the process. I crept along the dirt roads around the Barnes estate, blasting Mrs. Barnes's voice through a PA speaker in the engine grill. This trick had only worked a few times, but when it did, the missing dog had been less than a mile from its house. Occasionally it flushed out other people's dogs or caused callous residents to call the police. Damn Scarsdale had ticketed me for noise pollution so many times that the next violation was going to earn me jail time. But if I delivered Kebo to Mrs. Barnes the reward was so good that I might never have to bother with Scarsdale again.

With the voice-calling trick a bust, I drove into the Village of Wellington and asked the guy at the liquor store if he carried Calvados. He showed me a couple of brands, but they didn't match my bottle. Then he looked at the price sticker and told me immediately that it was from a store in Sharon, Connecticut, just over the state line.

When I got there, a pudgy man with blue five o'clock shadow was locking up.

"Excuse me, sir," I said.

"Closed," he said.

"I just need to ask you a question, sir."

"Hey! Did your mother drop you on your head? I'm closed!"

"Sir, it involves a missing dog."

"I don't care if it involves a missing sack of gold. I'm going home."

I showed him the Calvados bottle. "I know you don't sell a lot of this. Who'd you sell it to? Tell me and I'll go away."

"No," he said, "you'll go away now."

He swung at me, but he was impossibly slow and I put the heavy glass bottle between my jaw and his fist.

"Ah, jiminy crickets!" He cradled his hand in his other hand. "You sonovabitch, you broke my hand!"

"*I* broke it? You swung at me. Just tell me who bought this."

"I don't know. Tall guy with a mustache. Paid cash. Drove a white van. That's all I know."

"Make and model on the van?"

"Screw you!"

"You're right, too much. Thanks for your help."

"You gotta take me to the hospital," he said. "Look at the swelling!"

"Oh, quit your bellyaching," I said. "You've still got one good hand."

Driving home, I reflected on how little progress I'd made. What did I know? A tall guy with a mustache bought a bottle of Calvados. I didn't even know if he was the same guy who left the bottle on Mrs. Barnes's property.

Turning off the Saw Mill Parkway into Chappaqua, I spotted a chocolate Lab running loose on the Reader's Digest campus. I pulled over, scrolled through the photo file on my iPhone and found a match. If this was him, his name was Barney. I jumped out with a Milk-Bone and a 5-foot animal control pole with an adjustable noose at the end, and followed the dog into the woods. It was twilight, and if I didn't catch him now, I might not get another chance.

I played its owner's voice on the phone: "Barney! Here, Barney! Come here Barn-Barn!"

The dog stopped and looked at me askance. I squatted and waved the Milk-Bone. *Looky here, boy!* I dropped it on the leaves and readied the noose.

This is always the critical moment. It's a contest between you and the dog—which of you is going to move first? I've developed an uncanny ability for stillness. The key is, you can't look too eager. Early in my dogcatching career, the canines could smell my desperation for the reward. You have to project nonchalance—a feeling that you can take them or leave them.

Barney licked his chops and walked in with his head hanging. Clearly, he was hungry and tired of running. As he nosed forward for the treat, I slipped the noose over his head, and he came along without a fight, jumping into the carrier in the back of the Jeep and curling up for a nap. It was almost as though other dogs had told him about me, the Dogcatcher, and that it was in his best interest to go with me. By the time I caught up to them, most of them were tired of running anyway.

When I showed up with Barney at his owner's house, the entire family poured onto the lawn screaming the dog's name. It was touching. Not so touching, though, that it stopped me from grabbing Dad by his robe and rubbing my fingers together.

Barney was a cool grand.

Catching Barney made me late to the vet's office, where Carmel worked as a tech. I parked in front, and as I walked around to the service entrance, I saw her through the window. She was shampooing a German Schnauzer. I stopped and watched her.

I met Carmel after Ursula and I had divorced, and I took a lot of flack from my female friends over her. She's a pale redhead with several tats and piercings, she's 15 years younger than me, and because her parents were notorious stoners they named her Carmel when her last name was Sunday. I hadn't expected to fall for her, but the heart wants what it wants, and it turns out she's incredibly wise for her age.

Her diamond nose stud glinted in the light. She smiled and said something to the dog as she scrubbed it with a brush. I quietly went inside and snuck down the hall. My plan was to come up behind her and cup her breasts, but I was foiled by the Schnauzer. The dog barked and jumped around in the sink, splashing on Carmel's lab coat.

"Help, Lucy," Carmel said, "it's a dirty dogcatcher!"

I kissed her neck. "Hungry?"

"Starved," she said. "Why, are you taking me out?"

"Better. I've got filet mignon."

Over dinner I told her about Kebo, and when she asked me how big the reward was, I said, "Big, baby-doll. Real big."

Talk of large sums of cash got both of us excited, and I was already plenty agitated from Mrs. Barnes's preternatural behind, so we finished our conversation in the bedroom—the only place I noticed the difference in our ages. After a couple rounds with Carmel, all I wanted to do was go to sleep. Meanwhile, she sat up, lit a joint and bounced with surplus energy.

"So, tell me again. How big is it?"

"Huge." I clutched my pillow thinking of all that money.

"And you think you'll find him?"

I rolled over and stared at her.

"Duh, what am I saying?" She gave me a kiss tinged with cannabis. "Of course you will. You're the dogcatcher!"

She got up nude and turned on a table lamp. In this light, the blonde, pink and purple streaks in her naturally flawless red hair sparkled like they had glitter in them. It wouldn't surprise me if it was glitter. I didn't always approve of the things she did to her body—Nature had blessed her bountifully and I didn't understand her seeming lack of gratitude—but I kept quiet about it.

"I'm getting ice cream," she said. "Want anything?"

"No, sweetie. I'm fine."

Carmel returned with a pint of Ben & Jerry's Pistachio Pistachio. The girl would eat the entire thing with no effect on her body whatsoever.

"So, do you think the reward might...you know, be enough for us to do that thing we've talked about? I only ask because I got a letter the other day saying my deferment is up, and I have to give them a decision."

"You should call and tell them yes."

"*Yes?*" She pounced on my back like a lioness on an antelope.

"Sure," I said. "And as soon as I find this dog and get paid, we'll go up to Ithaca and look around."

"Omigod, that would be so awesome! A real college visit. Can we stay overnight?"

"Of course. We'll have to. It's like five hours up there."

"A nice hotel. With a hot tub. And can we take a tour and everything? I mean, I know it's silly, but—"

"Anything you want, Carmel. Let's go to sleep now. I have to find the dog first."

She sniffed. I could hear her crying.

"Don't cry, sweetie."

"You're wonderful," she said. "My parents never did anything for me."

"I know."

Really, the girl was amazing. Not only had she gotten herself out of a podunk New Hampshire town, she'd also put herself through college *and* been accepted to Cornell for veterinary school. She kissed my shoulder, wetting it with her tears.

"Do you think I'll be a good vet?"

"The best, kid. The best."

I was fortifying myself with a big breakfast at the White Plains Diner. The second day was always the longest, and with the shorter autumn days, I needed to get in as much daylight searching as possible. The waitress was refilling my coffee when my phone rang. The second I picked up, Mrs. Barnes fired into me like a Federal prosecutor.

"Are you on the job yet?"

"I'm heading up there in a few minutes," I said.

"Well, don't bother. He's back."

"What?" The cup slipped out of my fingers, spilling coffee across the table. "What do you mean he's back?"

"A couple of men found him last night and brought him to me a few minutes ago. He's fine. I wanted to tell you before you drove all the way up here. You can keep the retainer, by the way."

"I'll be there in an hour," I said. "Don't go anywhere."

When I got there, Mrs. Barnes and Kebo were climbing into the Range Rover.

"Wait," I said. "I need to talk to you."

"I'm sorry, but I have places to be today," she said.

"I just need a moment." I rapped on the passenger's door, where Kebo was curled up on the seat, panting. "Can I take a look at the dog?"

"Go ahead."

I opened the door and let the dog sniff me. Friendly enough. He didn't look harmed in any way. I examined his paws. If Sherlock Holmes did this, he'd find mud that could be traced to one place in a hundred miles. I didn't find so much as a pebble.

"The guys that returned him," I said. "Did they give you their names?"

"Ed and Frank."

"No last names?"

"No, and I didn't care. They brought Kebo *back*. That was enough for me. Now I really have to go. Kebo has a spa date."

"What did they look like?"

"One was short and balding, the other was tall with a mustache. They were both in their fifties, I'd say."

I was petting the dog. His collar was crooked, so I straightened it out. There was a black box attached to it next to his ID tag.

"You know, Mrs. Barnes, " I said, "you could have told me Kebo had a tracking collar. It would have saved both of us a lot of time."

"He didn't have one. They told me they put one on him so I wouldn't lose him again."

I shook my head and smiled. These guys were clever.

"What?" she said. "What's going on?"

"I'm not sure yet. But don't let Kebo out of your sight until I say it's okay." I rubbed the dog's head. "By the way, Mrs. Barnes, were they driving a white van by any chance?"

"Yes, I think it was white."

"That makes sense."

"Wait a minute." She shut off the engine and leaned across the passenger seat. "What are you saying?"

"You got hustled, Mrs. Barnes. I'm almost certain that the men that brought Kebo back are the same ones that took him."

"You're kidding."

"No, I'm not kidding. You didn't pay them the full reward, did you?"

She sighed.

"In cash?" I asked.

Her jaw clenched.

"All right," I said. "I'll be in touch."

————◆————

The only lead I had was that one of the men who returned the dog (if it was the same guy) had bought a bottle of Calvados from a Sharon, Connecticut liquor store. A lame clue, even for a dogcatcher. I got a couple of roast beef sandwiches at a deli on the way and tucked the Jeep into a corner of the parking lot with a clear view of the liquor store entrance. It was more than a long-shot—it was a full-court Hail Mary at the buzzer. Still, there was a chance they'd come back for their precious Calvados. I also had the tracking collar, which gave me an idea. I called Carmel.

"Hey, sexy," I said. "What are you wearing?"

"A smock. What's up?"

"I'm looking at one of those GPS pet tracking collars. If I give you the info on it, could you look it up and find out what you can for me?"

"Find out what?"

"Like where it was sold, to whom, that sort of thing."

"I'll try," she said. "Go ahead."

I read her the tiny print underneath the black box.

"So, are you getting close?" she asked.

"In a way."

"I love you, baby."

"You too, Red. Call me back."

Staring at the liquor store, I shared the sandwiches with Hunter and kept asking myself, "Why?" Stealing the dog for the reward I could understand, but why the tracking device?

"Why, Hunter?" He sat up and licked his chops.

Of course. To double-dip. If you found a sucker who paid the kind of reward Mrs. Barnes was offering, you'd want a chance to get it again. And to make sure of that, you'd need to keep tabs on the dog's whereabouts, so you'd know the best time to make the snatch.

Business was slow for the liquor store. Three people in two hours. Still, it was the middle of the day in the middle of the workweek. Only the leisure class and functioning alcoholics bought booze at this hour.

But how had they gotten into Mrs. Barnes's place? Apparently my subconscious had been giving this some thought. Either May Lee had sold out Kebo for a cut of the reward, or the dog-nappers had bribed somebody at the security company.

I had to take a leak, but I needed to keep the liquor store in sight. With my luck, the second I left the Jeep, they'd show up. The parking lot abutted some woods. From there, I'd have a view of the walkway in front of the stores. I got out with Hunter on his leash and had just sidled up to a maple tree when my phone rang. It was Carmel.

"What'd you get?" I asked.

"Zilch. How about you? Making any progress?"

I was staring in the direction of the liquor store when Hunter barked and a tall guy with a mustache stepped out from behind a tree. He was pointing a gun.

"Yeah, some," I said. "Talk to you later."

I put the phone in my pocket but didn't hang up. Then I felt a horrible thump on the back of my head and the world went dark.

--------◆--------

I came to with the sound of dogs barking all around me. Every range of bark—from shrill yips to baritone woofs. My head throbbed. I lay on cement with a drain under my elbow. I was surrounded by chain-link fencing. A kennel. I was in a kennel cage.

"Hey, he's up," said a man's voice.

"So?" said another.

"So…what are we going to do with him?"

"I don't know. I gotta think. We shouldn't of brought him here, Carlo."

My eyes adjusted to the harsh fluorescent lighting, and I made out several dogs I'd been looking for for weeks: Heloise, the Pomeranian; Buster, the black Lab; Annie, the Irish setter; Riley, the English springer spaniel; and Nugget, the Jack Russell terrier. Each of them represented a "SUBSTANTIAL REWARD." No wonder my business had dried up; the dogs weren't lost—these scumbags were nabbing them, then "finding" and returning them to their owners for the reward money.

There was the sound of footsteps, and then the two of them were staring at me through the cage.

"Hey," I said, "where's my dog?"

"He's here," Baldie said. "And don't worry, we fed him. The good stuff, too—Science Diet. Not that IAMS crap."

"How kind of you."

"We're businessmen, not animals."

I nodded at Mustache Man. "So, you must be Carlo—the one that likes Calvados. You two are real pieces of work, you know that? Kidnapping dogs."

Carlo hooked his fingers through the chain-link and leaned against the cage.

"We're not so different than you, buddy. I was hearing about you for a year, about this dogcatcher that was collecting these fat rewards, and that's when I got the idea for this. We're just doing what you do, with a little twist. It's a pretty slick deal, you gotta admit."

"Yeah, you're a genius," I said. "How do you get into the houses? You know people in the security companies, right?"

"Hey, Carlo," Baldie said, "this guy's pretty sharp."

"So, let me guess—now you're going to kill me," I said.

"Nah. Carlo's gonna beat you with a stick. Alls we want to do is *dissuade* you—you know, from talking."

Carlo grabbed a half-broomstick and started to open the lock. I backed up against the cage. The moment he got the lock off, there was a whizzing sound in the air, and he collapsed. A dart stuck out of his ass cheek.

"What the fu—?" Baldie said, and then he fell, too.

Footsteps echoed. A moment later Carmel walked in wearing her paratrooper boots and a leather jacket, and carrying a tranquilizer gun. She kicked Carlo in the leg. Nothing happened.

"They'll be out for a while," she said.

"Wow, you've never looked hotter to me," I said.

She opened my cage and we kissed. We kissed for a long time.

"How'd you find me?" I asked.

"Tracked your phone online," she said. "I also heard a lot before the connection crapped out."

I got down on one knee and searched their pockets.

"What are you looking for?" she asked.

"This." I pulled out two baseball-sized knots of $100 bills. "I'm going to give it back to Mrs. Barnes."

"But what about—"

"Relax, sweetie. Look…"

I waved my hand down the length of the loud and smelly kennel. There had to be at least 50 cages in here, which meant at least 50 rewards. And they were all sure to be "SUBSTANTIAL"; otherwise, these guys wouldn't have bothered with them. Carmel bounced up and down.

"Oh, but wait." She nodded at the men on the floor. "What do we do with *them* while we return the dogs?"

"Easy."

I tied them up in separate cages, taped their mouths, and borrowed their van for the dog deliveries. It took us two solid days and ten trips, but in the end the individual rewards for the dogs were more than the one for Kebo alone.

When we finished, I left Carlo and Baldie tied up and called the state police. The evidence and all of the dogs' owners' contact information was on the floor next to the crooks, along with a note from me:

"These two are responsible for a spate of dog-nappings over the past couple of months. All of the dogs have been returned to their rightful owners. — The Dogcatcher."

THE LOST DISPATCHES OF GENERAL GEORGE B. MCCLELLAN

On April 12, 2011—the sesquicentennial of the start of the Civil War—in a bricked-up Trenton, New Jersey wall safe, a cache of lost letters, telegrams and military dispatches from George B. McClellan, Union Major-General, was discovered. Historians had hoped this new evidence would exonerate the General of 150-year-old accusations of self-deception, jealousy, finger-pointing, paranoia, pomposity, overcautiousness, insubordination, and gross incompetence. Authored from when he took command of all Union forces in 1861, through his Peninsular Campaign of 1862, until relieved of command late that fall, these lost documents are remarkably revealing. It is believed that President Lincoln and Secretary of War Stanton, as well as McClellan's devoted wife, suppressed these documents so as not to alarm the nation.

———◆◆◆———

My Present Location: WASHINGTON, July 29, 1861

> My Darling Nelly[1],
> Of a modern Major-General, I am the very model. My that has a pleasant ring to it! Once I have saved the Union from this notorious Rebel uprising, I shall

---

1 McClellan's wife, Mary Ellen.

commission a play about myself &[2] make the writer include that line in my character's soliloquy.

The Army I have inherited is in a dreadful state: depressed, slouching & shoeless after their defeat at Bull Run. To remedy the situation I am planning a fierce campaign of recruitment, drill & crisp new uniforms—not to mention several morale-raising parades.

I regret that I must cut this letter short, as I have a Council of War with Old Fuss n' Feathers & the Original Gorrilla [sic].[3] Tomorrow's moon shall not bathe your cheek before I write again.

Lovingly yours,
The General

NEW YORK, NY, November 20, 1861

Hon. Simon Cameron, SECRETARY OF WAR:[4]
I wire you from New York, where I am attending to urgent personal business before the spring campaign gets underway. My recent promotion to General-in-Chief & Commander of the Army of the Potomac leaves me little free time for the minutiae of Life. Would you inquire with the Quartermaster General about something? I am still waiting for my new calling cards & stationary [sic], not to mention the brass plate for my Headquarters office door. — Geo. B. McClellan, General-in-Chief, Major-General, Commanding, Army of the Potomac.

---

2 McClellan had a inexplicable love of ampersands, using them instead of the word "and" in all correspondence.

3 General-in-Chief Winfield Scott and President Abraham Lincoln.

4 This message was translated from an original telegraph tape. In all likelihood, the War Department telegrapher was embarrassed by the message and therefore never bothered to transcribe it.

WASHINGTON, February 4, 1862

To His Excellency the PRESIDENT:
I recently heard of the King of Siam's offer of war Elephants to the Union Army & of your declining the offer. I beg you, Sir, to reconsider, as I am certain that a herd of armor-plated, stampeding Elephants at the head of this advancing army would cause mass panic in the Rebels' ranks & bring about their mass surrender. In the meantime they could be used to entertain the troops between engagements, & after the Grand Decisive Battle, the surviving elephants could be sold to P.T. Barnum.

Mr. President, I think the King's elephants could prove to be veritable manna from Heaven. Please reply at your soonest. If here when operations begin, I could use them.[5]

In response to your laundry-list of questions regarding my battle plan for the Peninsula, allow me to say that not only is my plan better than your Overland idea, it will prove to be twice the fun.

Your obedient servant,
Geo. B. McClellan, General-in-Chief, Major-General, Commanding, Army of the Potomac

---

WASHINGTON, March 12, 1862

Mr. PRESIDENT:
I have been in a morass of melancholy since yesterday when I read your "Special" War Order No. 3

---

5 This sentence is a dangling modifier. It is unclear whether the General meant "If *the elephants* are here..." or "If *I* am here...";
however, given his use of the objective case pronoun "them," as well as his habit of remaining stationary, it is likely that he meant the following: "If [the elephants are] here when operations begin, I could use them."

relieving me of my position as General-in-Chief. I do not understand. Do you not recall when I said I could do it all? Because I can, you know. This is humiliating. The press are already doing cartwheels over it. I wish you would reconsider. Command of the Army of the Potomac by itself seems so small now.

Respectfully,

Geo. B. McClellan, ~~General-in-Chief,~~ Major-General, Commanding, Army of the Potomac

---

FORT MONROE, VA, April 2, 1862

Hon. E.M. Stanton, SECRETARY OF WAR:

The armada has landed. I plan to stay aboard my flagship for a couple of days before proceeding inland. Need a good shave, & onboard will likely be my last hot bath for some time. Please relate the above to the President as I have resolved not to speak with him for a while.

—Geo. B. McClellan, Major-General, Commanding.

THE PENINSULA, April 3, 1862

To the Brooks Brothers Company, Broadway, New York, NY

Dear Messrs. Brooks:

This morning I received your parcel of March 20—the express shipment of the gold epaulets & sabre sash for my Full Dress Uniform. They are *abominable*. You will recall that last November I suspended my reorganizing operations for the Army of the Potomac & ventured north to New York City in one of the Gunboats at my disposal, so as to be properly fitted by your firm, which I had always viewed as a maker of the highest quality dress garments for Very Important Gentlemen, such as myself. I am now persuaded of the opinion that your team of tailors is actually a tribe of troglodytes.

Let us consider the sash. Not only is the sash 13-&-one-quarter inches too long, draping across my nethers like a savage's loincloth, but there are sixty-seven strands of gold fringe on each end, rendering each strand wispy & effeminate. This, after I expressly specified no more than forty-six strands & no fewer than forty-four. The sash, my dear Sirs, is useless to me; altho' given its hyperbolic length, I may keep it; if capture by the Rebels were ever imminent, I should prefer to hang myself with it, rather than be caught dead wearing it.

Whereas President Lincoln will be reviewing the Army (at a time & location yet to be disclosed), I insist that with all possible haste you tailor a new sash & epaulets to my specifications & place them on the New York–Washington Special Train, which is at the disposal of the Army General Staff. One of my 11 orderlies or 19 aides-de-camp will meet your courier at the station & conduct the goods by gunboat to our Secret Location on the Peninsula. Please confirm by telegraph. If the line is busy, keep trying.

Inasmuch as you value me as a continued Brooks Brothers customer, & inasmuch as you value continued contracts with the United States War Department as the official vendor of uniform accoutrements & splendiferies for the Army General Staff, do *not* fail me.

Upbraidingly yours,
George B. McClellan, Major-General, Commanding

SOMEWHERE ON THE PENINSULA, April 5, 1862

To his Excellency the PRESIDENT:

We are settling in quite comfortably here on the Peninsula, altho' it is unpredictably rainy & the air miasmically steamy. The Corps of Engineers did a marvelous job of razing a swath through the woods &

swamps, & building a corduroy road with felled trees stretching from Fort Monroe to our secret encampment miles inland.

There is much unique flora & fauna in this country. Knowing your appreciation of novelties, Sir, enclosed with this dispatch you will find a most singular butterfly—its wings, as you will note, are the precise colors of our flag, albeit in a far more sage configuration, owing to the Divine Wisdom of our most Heavenly Creator. I consider this beautiful insect to be an omen, a sign from Providence that our cause is just & has His blessing. As you see, my Adjutant-General went to great pains to secure the live butterfly (*without* a proper net) & gently insert it in this bottle; however, being ignorant as to what the creature eats, we contained it without sustenance, so it has likely perished during the journey to Washington.

Your obedient servant,

George B. McClellan, Major-General, Commanding

OUTSIDE OF YORKTOWN, VA, April 7, 1862

Mr. PRESIDENT:

In my last dispatch, I neglected to inform you as to the Army's activity, so here it is:

The force we are facing is considerable, & I would be traitorous if I did not apprise you of this fact. Yesterday I observed through a break in the trees a continual stream of gray uniforms pouring into their camp, & my forward observers, including Mr. Pinkerton, confirmed this steady flow of men. This deluge continued all day, so I should estimate we have at least 200,000 men in front of us—twice my number. Perforce, more troops for this army are needed. A *lot* more.

Altho' the Rebels are camped less than two miles distant, there have been no actual engagements as yet.

There have been skirmishes, however. Yesterday evening, just as the gloaming enveloped the countryside & the mourning doves began to coo, shots rang out from our center. I immediately sent out a rider to ascertain their cause. Returning, he reported that a dozen or so Rebels had been captured. When questioned they admitted that their paltry attack was completely unsanctioned; the Rebel band was simply bored, they said.

Clearly, my strategy of amassing an Army in close proximity to the Rebels & then unnerving them by simply waiting here is working. I am increasingly convinced that excellent Union entrenchments and a few splendid marches will be enough to make the enemy throw down their arms, thus preventing further bloodshed.

The Rebel captives also contended that their force around Yorktown is tiny & that it only *seems* large. They claim that their commander, General John B. Magruder, has been marching the same troops in circles in sight of my observers, so as to give the impression of a massive army. This, of course, is a false subterfuge.[6] The Rebel soldiers have no doubt been instructed to tell us this lie if captured, hoping to lure my Army to its total destruction. Well, nice try, Rebels, but McC isn't falling for it.

As I am sure it is clear to a man of your wisdom, Mr. President, my campaign of seeming inaction is not without its reasons. The great ancient Chinese warlord Sun Tzu (Sun Soo) wrote that all war is based on deception. It is my intention to deceive the Rebels into a sense of false security, much like a fly in a tavern. By seeing this Army behaving in such a quiet,

---

6 No, it's true: Magruder's force totaled about 11,000; McClellan's, 110-120,000. Knowing he was outnumbered 10 to 1, Magruder, an amateur theater impresario, put his theatrical bent to good use by parading the same troops endlessly in front of McClellan's observers. This *ad hoc* maneuver delayed McClellan for weeks, causing him to entrench his men and begin an unnecessary siege of Yorktown.

unobtrusive & conciliatory manner, our Confederate neighbors will not expect an all-out assault when the right time comes. And it is coming soon, I assure you. As soon as we have overwhelming superiority of men & matériel, we will swat the enemy just as an annoyed tavern-keep would swat said fly.

I must attend to my afternoon inspection of the lines, Mr. President, so I beg leave of you.

Your obedient servant,

George B. McClellan, Major-General, Commanding

OUTSIDE YORKTOWN, VA, April 8, 1862

Hon. E.M. Stanton, SECRETARY OF WAR:

A brief cable to alert you that I have ordered the building of fortifications for a siege of Yorktown. As you may know, I am a great fan of the siege. We shall have marvelous moats, truculent trenches, ravaging ramparts, and winning wooden obstructions! Clearly, the enemy forgets that the great George Washington trapped Cornwallis here, & by siege compelled his surrender. I require the siege guns with the 200-pound shells to drive them out of there. Throw in a couple dozen of the 13-inch seacoast mortars as well. Must attend to preparations. My God, is there anything as thrilling as a good siege?! —Geo. B. McClellan, Major-General, Commanding

---

THE PENINSULA, April 12, 1862

To the E. & H. T. Anthony Studios, 501 Broadway, New York, NY

Messrs. Anthony:

You will recall that last November I visited your studios & you took some 200 photos of me. Please forward a print of the "stereoview" picture of me in my field uniform (No. 6278) to Highgate & White, Architects, Chicago, Ill. Time is of the essence. You may send it on the New York–Chicago Army Special Train. Present this telegram as your ticket. Good for 7 days, non-transferrable. I am depending upon you. —Geo. B. McClellan, Major-General, Commanding.

———————◆•◆•◆————————

THE PENINSULA, April 12, 1862

To: Highgate & White, Architects, Chicago, Ill.
Gentlemen:
I should like to retain your firm for the design & construction of a house. I require accommodations more befitting a man of my station, said accommodations also serving as my Head Quarters here at my Secret Location here on the Peninsula.

I leave the actual design to your firm; however, the house must include certain features. These are non-negotiable:

1. The house must be portable. By "portable," I mean that it could either be dragged on a giant sledge by ten to twelve teams of mules, or it can be disassembled, moved on train flatcars & reassembled at a new location in a matter of hours.

2. The first floor must include a giant Map Room, with a map of the entire United States (including those states in Rebellion) printed on the floor & surrounded by rails, & long shuffleboard sticks with which to maneuver scale models of our Armies. There must also be a bar with gleaming brass rails, a walk-in humidor with compartments for each officer's personal cigars, & a telegrapher's nook.

3. The bannister post at the foot of the stairs should be a carved image of my head (for some sense of depth, use forthcoming "stereoview" photo from the E. & H. T. Anthony Studios of New York). Mahogany would be ideal; oak is acceptable.

These are my only requirements, gentlemen. Please remit the invoice to E.M. Stanton, Secretary of War.

Cordially Yours,
George B. McClellan, Major-General, Commanding, Army of the Potomac

P.S.: I need it here next Tuesday.
P.P.S.: All further correspondence, including the house, may be shipped to my newly opened Post Office. Please note, my address has changed: The General, P.O. Box 1, Secret Location, The Peninsula, Virginia.

YORKTOWN SIEGEWORKS, VA, April 15, 1862

Hon. E.M. Stanton, SECRETARY OF WAR:
Send whiskey (the good stuff). Orderlies' and Adjutant-General's nerves are shot. Otherwise all is fine.
—Geo. B. McClellan, Major-General, Commanding.

YORKTOWN, VA, May 4, 1862

To his Excellency the PRESIDENT:
I have taken Yorktown with nary a shot. My batteries were about to open fire when it was discovered that Magruder & his men abandoned the place last night. Can you believe it? In addition to some excellent fried chicken in their HQ, they left several "Quaker Guns"[7] behind, clearly trying to convince me they were poorly armed so I would attempt direct assaults against their future positions. Silly Rebels. Next stop, Williamsburg. Wish me luck. —Geo. B. McClellan, Major-General, Commanding.

---

7 Logs attached to wheels, designed to resemble cannon from a distance.

WILLIAMSBURG, VA, May 6, 1862

To the PRESIDENT of the United States:
Williamsburg is ours! We did a number on the place, but it serves the Rebels right. In the years since Virginia luminaries like Washington & Jefferson graced these streets, they have turned this place into a Colonial theme park. The ticket prices are outrageous! If you do not think it a waste of good ordnance, am seriously considering blowing up the entire town. This is too good a revenue stream for the Confederacy. Please advise Yea or Nay on the blow-up plan.
—Geo. B. McClellan, Major-General, Commanding.

HEADQUARTERS, ARMY OF THE POTOMAC, May 16, 1862.

To General A.P. Hill, Army of Northern Virginia
Sir:
My contacts at Tiffany & Co. of Fifth Avenue in New York City inform me that a Southern gentleman known only as "A.P." ordered a cameo to be delivered to one Mary Ellen Marcy. That woman, Sir, is my wife.

I warn you, if you attempt to court Mary Ellen again, after you played the game and lost, I shall be forced to call you out.[8] Yes, a *duel*. I have agents inter-

---

8 Before the war, A.P. Hill had asked for beautiful Mary Ellen Marcy's hand, but her father objected to the match. Hill had no money, was only a lieutenant, and on top of everything else he was a Southerner. But when George McClellan, then a vice-president of the Illinois Central Railroad, proposed to Mary Ellen, Mr. Marcy pushed her to marry him. According to legend, A.P. Hill never forgot that McClellan stole Mary Ellen. Anytime his forces were near McClellan's—which, during the Peninsular Campaign, was often—they fought vociferously.

cepting the mail, and your "gift" will be readdressed from me to Mrs. Lincoln.

Do not try me, Sir,

G.B. McClellan, Major-General, Commanding, Army of the Potomac

---

THE PENINSULA, May 17, 1862

Dearest Nelly, my Little Presbyterian[9],

I see the News papers have begun to refer to me deridingly as "The Virginia Creeper" because of my careful, measured progress up the Peninsula. These "war correspondents"—these hollow, unpatriotic snipes—are useless. They are my sworn enemies.

What they fail to grasp is that one of the definitions of the infinitive "to creep" is this: "to sneak up behind someone or without someone's knowledge," which is exactly what I am attempting to do with this moving city of over 100,000 men & 14,000 animals. It is by no means easy.

If these ridglings[10] wish to be pedantic, directing their insipid attack instead on the noun "creeper," then I proffer this definition: "any of various tools or implements designed to assist a man, animal, or machine to advance or climb." As Colonel Smithers, my geometry professor at West Point, said daily, "*Quod erat demonstrandum.*"

My dear, sweet Nelly, I hope always to shield you from the seething, burning rage in my heart that wishes these men ground into dust, doused in turpentine & set aflame. I will do my best to remain Christian towards them & the legions of other detractors conspiring against me.

---

9 One of his pet names for Mary Ellen. Yeah, we know—weird.

10 An antiquated term in today's horseless age: "a male animal in which one or both testes have not descended into the scrotum."

Stay well. I hope your tulips are beginning to blossom—the pink ones. They are a delight.

Most affectionately,
The General

RICHMOND'S DOORSTEP, May 20, 1862

Mr. PRESIDENT:

I am dictating this wire from *U.S.A.S.S.* (United States Air Ship Supreme) *Envisage*, a gaseous ball-loon [sic] that comprises the latest technological innovation in our fight against Rebel terrorizm [sic]. We are most fortunate that I had the imagination & foresight to realize the value of Professor Thaddeus Lowe's Ball-loon [sic] Corps as an instrument for obtaining intelligence against the enemy.[11] From this great height, with a spyglass, our reconnaissance officers can see in a 50-mile radius on a clear day. Today, Mr. President, if you were to run up to the White House roof & wave a flag, I would probably be able to see you too.

After a mishap yesterday, the Ship has been better secured. The rope broke during my first trip aloft, casting me, Professor Lowe & the telegrapher to the wind. Rebel cavalry (J.E.B. Stuart) took chase as we sailed toward Richmond, some 8 miles distant. With their left flank suddenly exposed, I scribbled a hasty order, fastened it to a sandbag & tossed it down to our own men in pursuit. The commander of Battery D walloped their flank with the new 200-pounders Secretary Stanton sent. Those are some sweet guns, Sir.

Looking out at the Rebel front now. The encampments seem to be for a force of 70,000, but Mr. Pinkerton assures me that the Rebels of necessity

---

11 This is patently false. McClellan, along with most of the Union generals, initially did not see the value in aerial reconnaissance balloons. In fact, it was President Lincoln who, on June 17, 1861, received the first aerial telegraph message from Lowe, and in late July (after Bull Run), hired Lowe to "begin at once."

sleep 8 to a tent instead of 2, putting their total force at no less than 280,000. I must have 150,000 reinforcements immediately.

Rebel artillery firing at our craft. Must descend.

—G. B. McC., Maj.-Gen., Cmdng.

THE PENINSULA, May 25, 1862

My Darling Nelly,

Your General misses you. He yearns to see you— you as bewitchingly beatific as the Sirens who so throbbingly tempted great Odysseus with their song. Indeed, whenever the General receives one of your violet-scented letters, with your sweet voice so clear & piquant, he requires one of his eleven orderlies lash him to his bed-posts so he will not crash the ship of his illustrious military career upon the perilous rocks of impropriety. As your revivifying & mesmeric words wash over him, all of him stiffens & he strains at the bonds which keep him here, at his Secret Location on the Peninsula.

The General wishes you to know that only a cause as grand as the restoration of this great Union could possibly impel him to continued separation from you. He dreams of the day when he can again brush your luxuriant hair & delicately varnish your tender toenails.

With *deepest* affection,

The General

NEAR RICHMOND, VA, June 1, 1862

Mr. PRESIDENT:

I regret your recently receiving a letter meant for my wife & ask for your understanding in this matter. Surely as a man who was away from home often as a young lawyer, you can appreciate the strong sentiments that motivated my missive.

In military action, my artillery commanders report our having lobbed no fewer than a hundred of the 200-pounders at General Joseph Johnston's forces yesterday. My aides & I are in disagreement as to what the fight should be named: the "Battle of Seven Pines" or "Fair Oaks." Which do you prefer, Mr. President? I prefer "Seven Pines" myself.

It seems Johnston was badly wounded & carried from the field. As you may know, Sir, he was a mentor of mine during the Mexican War, so I am rather saddened at this news. If Davis is smart, he'll put Lee in there, but I've got Lee's number.[12]

Your obedient servant,
Geo. B. McClellan, Major-General, Commanding.

A LITTLE CLOSER TO RICHMOND, VA, June 3, 1862

Mr. PRESIDENT:

As you probably know, my early service was in the Corps of Engineers—training that I put to some use yesterday against the Enemy. I designed & supervised the construction of an enormous, oxen-powered air-propellor, or fan, to blow the savory smells of our hickory-smoked bacon across the Enemy's front. As you can imagine, Sir, bacon is the coin of the realm in these parts. My most ingenious Fan will no doubt have the effect of surrender *en masse* that I have always presaged. Yet, the tactic gives me a twinge of guilt as some of my West Point comrades are over there, & the thought of their subsisting on nothing but salt pork & corn pone makes me ill. However, from the moment you put me in command of this great Army, I have used all means at my disposal to put an end to this insurrection, & teasing the Rebels with mouth-watering fare is one of them.

---

12 Robert E. Lee *was* put in command of the Army of Northern Virginia from this point until the end of the war, and McClellan *didn't* have his number.

Also, Mr. President, I take offense to your recent denial of my request for reinforcements. As justification for your denial, you cited the 121,800 who were "present for duty" at the start of this campaign; however, as the following chart clearly shows, that number is terribly inaccurate; as a military term, "present for duty" means squat. To wit,

Total number of officers and soldiers "present for duty" at start of Peninsula Campaign (approx.)	**121,800**
Deduct men in jail	4,200
Deduct unarmed & unequipped men	6,340
Deduct men eating meals (various)	25,002
Deduct non-fighting men (cooks, priests, farriers, orchestra, photographers, ball-loon inflaters, paymasters, telegraphers, theatre troupes, tap-dancers, other)	15,208
Deduct men too drunk or hung-over to fight	33,124
Deduct cavalry (no idea where they are most of the time)	17,006
Deduct men with recently lost limbs who need naps	5,087
Deduct men with sloppy uniforms (or missing buttons)	9,264
Deduct men posing for photographs	2,433
Deduct men who are "otherwise engaged"	2,700
Actual Number of Men Available for Fighting	**1,436**

Little activity on the lines this week. Two skirmishes & some random shots by our own troops at late-returning northbound geese.

Your obedient servant,

Geo. B. McClellan, Major-General, Commanding

P.S.: You grew up poor, Mr. President; what *is* corn pone anyway? I need to know!

HEADQUARTERS, ARMY OF THE POTOMAC, June 6, 1862.

> To General A.P. Hill, Army of Northern Virginia
> Sir:
> Be advised—one of my agents intercepted your cameo before it could reach its intended recipient. I find your recent denial of this affair highly amusing, given the inscription on the piece, which reads, "Nelly—I am forever yours, A.P." This engraving making it impossible to re-gift it to Mrs. Lincoln, by my order the cameo was hurled into the Potomac. Any other "gifts" will suffer the same fate.
> Make no more attempts to correspond with Mrs. *McClellan*. If I chance upon you in battle, Sir, I will have your hide.
> —George McClellan

THE PENINSULA, June 9, 1862

> Dearest Nelly,
> My love, I hope this telegram finds you in good health & spirits. We are to make a move soon, so I am pressed for time. Just know that I am well & thinking of you. Also, could you please send my whale bone mustache comb with all possible haste? I expect the Original Gorrilla [sic] to make a surprize [sic] inspection any day now, & my normally manicured mustache resembles a swamp thicket. With all possible love—The General.

THE PENINSULA, June 16, 1862

To the Boston & Vienna Piano Company, Ltd., Boston, Mass.

Gentlemen:

As you are no doubt aware, since reports of the exploits of the Army of the Potomac have been laudatory & copious, I am the Commander of this grand assemblage of men. In this capacity, besides endeavoring to field the bravest fighting force, & besides developing strategies to smite the Rebel forces with the least possible damage to this Army (which I now hold quite dear), I have taken it upon myself to inspire, motivate & extend the cultural education of my soldiers through music. This is where your company can be of great service to the Union.

I am looking to acquire a new grand piano forte for the Army. Our last one sunk in a bog, rendering it unplayable. You may ship the piano here (send a full-time piano tuner with the instrument; Army travel wreaks havoc on pianoes [sic]) & remit the invoice to Mr. Stanton, Secretary of War.

Yours,

George B. McClellan, Major-General, Commanding

NEAR RICHMOND, VA, June 22, 1862

Hon. E.M. Stanton, SECRETARY OF WAR:

My sentries, spies & other forward observers inform me that we are facing an entrenched Rebel force around Richmond of no less than 350,000 men. I now require 250,000 reinforcements. Thanks!

—Geo. B. McClellan, Major-General, Commanding.

NEAR RICHMOND, VA, June 23, 1862

Mr. PRESIDENT::

I received your recent & rather curt wire in which you expressed exasperation over my seeming inaction. As I have noted countless times, Sir, my experience as a professional soldier, if nothing else, has taught me this: Constant marching on muddy roads among the horseflies, & bloodying the troops' uniforms in battle, erodes morale. If you will but be patient with me, Sir, I know you will find me to be in the right. —Geo. B. McClellan, Major-General, Commanding.

GAINES' MILL, VA, June 27, 1862

Hon. E.M. Stanton, SECRETARY OF WAR:

Under fierce attack by Lee's forces. Earlier enemy troop estimates grossly inaccurate. I have once again employed Mr. Pinkerton in the surreptitious acquisition of some most alarming data. New intelligence now indicates that we face a Rebel army of 900,000. This is a catastrophe! All northern males, of whatever age (the old ones can rip train tickets), should be sent immediately from Boston, New York City, Philadelphia & Chicago. If my calculations are correct, this measure would give me an army of 1,073,632 men. —Geo. B. McClellan, Major-General, Commanding.

SAVAGES [sic] STATION, VA, June 29, 1862

Hon. E.M. Stanton, SECRETARY OF WAR:

Add to my previous list all males from second-tier cities including Baltimore, Springfield (Ill.), Buffalo,

Hartford & Providence. Bolstering our forces from all of the aforementioned cities will give me an army of one & one-half million men. That should do the trick. P.S.: Send coffee. We're almost out. —Geo. B. McClellan, Major-General, Commanding.

TURKEY BRIDGE, VA, June 30, 1862

Hon. E.M. Stanton, SECRETARY OF WAR:
Another day of desperate fighting. We are hard pressed by superior numbers that seem to be coming from all directions. I fear I shall be forced to abandon my material to save my men under cover of the gunboats. Load all of the aforementioned city-dwellers onto barges & float them to Fort Monroe—fast! Meanwhile, I'll try to save the army. —Geo. B. McClellan, Major-General, Commanding.

TURKEY BRIDGE, VA, June 30, 1862

Hon. E.M. Stanton, SECRETARY OF WAR:
Almost forgot. Send more gunboats. —Geo. B. McClellan, Major-General, Commanding.

HARRISON'S LANDING (STILL ON THE PENINSULA), VA, July 10, 1862

Dear Nelly,
I apologize for neglecting to write the past two days, but the Great Baboon arrived unannounced on the 8th & I was forced to play host. He condescended to offer me, *George B. McClellan*, suggestions on strategy & tactics, to which I was sorely tempted to reply, "Did you graduate from West Point second in

your class, *too*, Mr. President?" However, I held my tongue & instead handed him as he left a blistering letter on the politics of the War (see how *you* like it, Abe), which he had the temerity to read in my presence, whereupon he folded it up & said two words: "All right." He then returned to Washington.

You know what I loathe most about the man? That *stupid* stove-pipe hat. As if he isn't tall enough already! And gnarly! The man is the indubitable offspring of a gorrilla [sic] and a telegraph pole. I shall write you again when I have calmed down from his intrusion.

With affection,
The General

THE PENINSULA, VA, July 12, 1862

To His Supreme Excellency the PRESIDENT:
Halleck? Halleck! You made HALLECK the new General-in-Chief? I would rather you installed General Lee in the position than that useless chromedome! The only thing Halleck is remotely good for is sharpening pencils, and even at that he is wanting. I believe you will regret this decision & wish you had kept McClellan in the post. —Geo. B. McClellan, Major-General.

STILL ON THE PENINSULA, August 5, 1862.

Dearest Nelly,
Well, the Great Baboon, through "Old S--t for Brains,"[13] has made his worst mistake yet—stripping me of my beloved Army of the Potomac, the Army *I* built, and giving it to that unmitigated chunk of

---

13 A shockingly rare expletive and a pejorative play on Halleck's nickname: "Old Brains."

driftwood, Pope.[14] At his suggestion, no doubt, they have given the force the *brilliant* new name of "the Army of Virginia." Pope is such an idiot, my darling, that if he ever gets an order from [Sec. of War] Stanton to destroy "the Army of *Northern* Virginia," he will ignore the adjective & direct his men to shoot each other, or themselves. I give him a month.[15]

I would resign were I not certain that the Gorrilla [sic], his zookeeper[16] and that horse-dung Halleck will eventually beg me to resume command. Oh, but if only so many Good Men did not have to die before these incompetents woke up and faced facts: that George B. McClellan is the best general they've got!

I have come under some scrutiny recently for my "questionable behavior" during the Battle of Malvern Hill, when I retired to one of the gunboats. Unfortunately, the duties of my position often require me to remain in the rear—an awful thing.

I must admit to showing a false countenance to the men, my dear, for while my heart smolders over this cruel and idiotic slight, I continue to exude an optimistic and indomitable air. In fact, this morning one of my aides said he was distressed at the Army losing "its head and constant champion," to which I replied with a rather smart retort: "I shall return."

Ah, but the silver lining in this is that we shall soon see a lot more of each other! Ready the household, my Love; the General is coming home.

Yours,
Brinton[17]

---

14 General John Pope.

15 On this point McClellan was remarkably prescient. Pope was appointed to command of the Army of Virginia on July 26, 1862, lost a couple of key battles (including Second Bull Run or Second Manassas), and by early September most of his forces were put back under McClellan's command.

16 Secretary of War Stanton.

17 McClellan's middle name. His using it displays a rare vulnerability.

SOME FARM IN MARYLAND, September 13, 1862

Nelly,

The General is back! Keep this under your bonnet, but I now have in my possession a document that, if genuine, could bring this war to a rapid & decisive close in a matter of days! It is Lee's "Special Orders No. 191," in which he spells out every detail of his battle plan for Maryland.[18] I have him now!

Do not fear for me & please do not neglect to dust my sabre scabbard—the one above the fireplace!

Faithfully yours,
The General

MARYLAND COUNTRYSIDE, September 14, 1862

Nelly,

Last night I gave serious thought to the windfall of Lee's plans. It occurred to me that it must be one of Lee's attempted psych-outs. The plans were wrapped around three cigars of Cuban origin & excellent quality, almost like bait for a bear trap. Undoubtedly the crafty old man drafted these bogus plans, which I am now going to ignore.

It is a delightful Injun Summer[19] here in the Maryland countryside. The foliage is marvelous. I wish you were here. I hope to have the Rebels mopped up in a

---

18 The order, drafted on or around September 9, 1862, gave specific details of the movements of the Army of Northern Virginia during the beginning of its invasion of Maryland. The most important piece of intelligence to be gleaned from the document was that Lee had divided his army, rendering the separate parts vulnerable.

19 Indian Summer.

couple of days, acquire Lee's surrender & come home to you victorious, darling. Pray for our noble Army.

With affection,

The General

———————◆•◆•◆———————

ANTIETAM CREEK, MD, October 3, 1862

Dearest Nelly,

Well, the President came out to visit, and even though I managed to wrangle a victory for the Union[20] against impossible odds, I am fairly certain that he is planning to replace me. He keeps nagging me about getting the Army "moving again." But the men are exhausted, and so am I. Will write again later. Need to see off the Baboon and take a nap.

Affectionately,

The General

———————◆•◆•◆———————

SALEM, VA, November 10, 1862

Nelly,

As you know from my previous correspondence, they took my beloved Army of the Potomac away from me. I have effectively been kicked out of the Army. I have no command now.

It is of mild condolence that my acquaintance, Burnside[21], was given the command. Let him try; maybe those ridiculous whiskers of his can win the war for us.

---

20 The "victory" was a Pyrrhic one at best. In fact, the final day of the battle—September 17, 1862—proved to be the bloodiest single day of fighting in American history: the Union had 12,401 casualties with 2,108 dead; Confederate casualties were 10,318 with 1,546 dead. Over 25,000 Americans killed, maimed or wounded.

21 Major-General Ambrose Burnside.

As I rode away, there were cheers from the men all along the line. Of course my detractors will claim the men were cheering because I was leaving; but if you could have seen the unrestrained joy in their faces & heard the hoarseness in their cheers, you would know, as I do, that their love is genuine.

I will see you soon.

With Love,

George

———————◆———————

For the rest of his life, George B. McClellan was revered by many veterans of the Army of the Potomac. Even his legions of critics were forced to agree that he had organized and built the Army, and that without his efforts the Army would likely have been decimated in any engagements following First Bull Run (or First Manassas). On October 29, 1885, aged 58, McClellan died unexpectedly of a heart attack. His final words were, "I feel easy now. Thank you."

The Charmed Life and Singular Death of Jacob Homer Stanley

Jacob Homer Stanley, a lifelong New England painter, died in faraway Sleeper, California of unknown causes. He was 39. While no scientific explanation was offered, one fact is obvious: Jacob's trouble began when he moved away from New England. It was as though something indigenous to those states had been his personal power source and when he was unplugged from it, he was drained of life.

Jacob's apparent physical connection to New England makes sense given his family's long history in the region. Far more than a Kennedy, a family that came late to the North American party, Jacob Stanley was by virtue of both his father's and mother's ancestries a veritable prince of New England. His first ancestor to America, Christopher Stanley, a tailor, arrived in Massachusetts Bay in 1635 on the Pilgrim ship *Elizabeth and Ann*. Subsequent generations remained in New England, becoming able-bodied seamen, coopers, cabinetmakers and stonecutters. Theirs was the humble branch of the Stanley family. More prominent Stanleys, including the founders of the hardware company, and the Stanley who slogged through the African jungles to heroically remark, *"Doctor*

Livingston, I presume?" were not from Jacob's line. Among all the Stanleys, Jacob was the first artist.

Jacob's mother's family, the Knowltons, arrived in New England in 1632. The most famous of them was Lieutenant Colonel Thomas Knowlton, of Connecticut, who served in the Revolutionary War as founder of the Rangers. He fought at Bunker Hill and died at the Battle of Harlem Heights, but luckily for Jacob Stanley had sired sons before his death. Generations later, a descendant of the Colonel, Thomas Anson Knowlton, made a decision that proved equally fortuitous for Jacob: he became a judge instead of his childhood dream of bush pilot. Years later he said to his grandson, Jacob, "Good thing I didn't become a flier. Would've ended up deader'n hell."

Jacob's father, John Stanley IV, had been bitten by a peculiar wanderlust bug that caused him to uproot his family annually, sometimes biannually, always resettling them somewhere in New England. By the time Jacob was 18 he had lived in two dozen towns in every state of the region. Despite the lack of stability in his life, or perhaps because of it, Jacob excelled as an artist. He also spent his childhood in near-perfect health, missing only eight days of school in 12 years, and only missing those days when, suspiciously, he became ill during trips outside of New England. But when he remained in his native region— the region that had been home to both sides of his family for over 350 years—he was impervious to illness.

After high school graduation, however, during a journey across the United States, Jacob got his first taste of sustained illness, with his conditions becoming more severe the farther he strayed from New England. Contact dermatitis in Philadelphia. Migraines in Chicago. A urinary infection in Taos, New Mexico. Tonsillitis in Vancouver. A subsequent trip abroad to study the masters was even worse, netting Jacob a herniated disc in London, a kidney stone in Paris and aseptic meningitis in Rome.

He returned to New England convinced that, for health reasons, he should never leave those 5½ states again (the western half of Connecticut, he learned, was iffy). He found an inexpensive studio—a crudely converted barn—in Cushing, Maine, down the road from painter Andrew Wyeth's summer home. Jacob painted 10 hours a day, walking the stony beaches at dawn and dusk, one evening passing Mr. Wyeth who was out doing the same. Flummoxed over what to say to the great man he blurted out, "Mr. Wyeth, I think you're a genius, sir!" Wyeth assumed an air of insecurity and mock surprise. "Gosh," he said, "you really think so?"

In fact, the notoriously reclusive Wyeth was touched and made a point of dropping by Jacob's studio. He praised the young man's execution but upbraided him about his grounding and use of poor quality materials.

"Pay the extra bucks now, kid," he said. "Steal the damn money if you have to, but use paints and canvases that are going to last. My stuff? They'll still be hanging my stuff four hundred years from now, when all of Pollock's automobile paint crap has long since saponified."

Taking the master's advice, Jacob invested in better materials. After a few more walks and studio chats he felt comfortable enough with Wyeth to mention his bizarre tendency to get sick anytime he left New England. Had Wyeth experienced anything similar? The old man was quiet for a minute, staring out the window at a ramshackle outhouse with a raspberry bramble grown up around it.

"Never mentioned it to anybody, especially Betsy," he said, "but if I'm not in Chadds Ford, or here in Cushing, or at least Downeast Maine someplace, something in me gets a little queasy. But diseases, like you're talking? No way. Give you a tip, Jacob. Never leave your easel and you'll never get sick. Might not die either. I plan to avoid it if I can."

Painting seascapes and portraits commissioned by wealthy summer people (from New York mostly), Jacob earned enough to keep him in good materials, thrift store clothing and occasional meals out at the Thomaston Cafe. Through Betsy Wyeth's influence, more prestigious collectors came calling and galleries in Portland started showing his work. When Jacob's *Owl's Head Fog* and *Fool Kids Swimming from Vinalhaven to North Haven* were featured in an exhibit at the Farnsworth Museum in Rockland, side-by-side with works by Andrew Wyeth, the art world took notice. Manhattan galleries began to feature him. His story of becoming, by Fate, a protégé of the curmudgeonly Wyeth was devoured by buyers. They thought it was the laying on of hands, when it was simply one painter bumping into another on a beach, and the two having coffee or a belt in the younger's studio.

The sudden exposure, heightened by a profile in *Down East* magazine, created unusual demand for his work, and because paintings sold better when collectors could meet the artist, Jacob had to attend four Manhattan shows in as many weeks. He was ill all four times (food poisoning, acid reflux, stomach virus, flu) before he arranged to have his paintings shown exclusively at a Martha's Vineyard gallery. He had no choice. New York City, for all its glitz and glorious charms—the scintillating restaurants; the cacophonous street noise, which on high floors became harmonious; the diaphanous summer morning light; and the roomfuls of elegant, aphrodisiacal women at parties (although he still preferred the rarer but far more earthy beauties of Maine)—despite all of New York's charms, he had to leave; it was literally making him puke.

And it was on the Vineyard, while walking the beach in front of his dealer's house, watching the sandpipers skitter away from the foam, that Jacob met the woman who would become his favorite model and the love of his life: Natalia Komissarzhevkaya. On her mother's side she descended from the great Russian writer Pushkin, but it was her father's lineage that was indirectly responsible for why Jacob ended up in California.

Two brothers, Dimitri and Sasha Komissarzhevkaya, were sick of living as serfs in Tsarist Russia. They had heard about a distant country called *United States*, where poor, pale men such as themselves didn't have to toil in fields for no wages. Such men could even own land if they wanted. *Land!*

One lush summer dawn, the two were gathering firewood in the trees on opposite sides of a field. A thin fog hovered above the grass. Loaded down with wood, the brothers were about to go home when two men rode up on horseback, dismounted and tore off their frock coats. Dimitri and Sasha knew what was coming: a duel.

The brothers crouched. Neither the men's seconds nor the physician had arrived yet. The two men began to argue about which coast of *United States* was better—East or West.

"The East has cities, culture, civilization," the taller one said.

"Ah," said the other, "but the West—this Republic of California—is a modern-day Eden, a perennially warm paradise where one can toss gold in the soil and see it grow. The only drawback is the boring sameness of the architecture."

"Not so of New York."

"I'm sick of your impudence." The tall one opened a box containing two pistols. "To hell with seconds. I wish to kill you now."

"Really, this is highly irregular, a breach of dueling etiquette," said the other, stroking his mustache. "But no matter. You shall die."

The Brothers K. watched from opposite sides of the clearing as the two duellers paced off, turned and fired, striking each other in the head. The duellers collapsed like scythed stalks of wheat. Dimitri and Sasha blinked at each other. Dumping their firewood, they approached the now-dead gentlemen. Both men's wallets contained identity papers and a great many rubles. Nodding to each other they quickly stripped the two men and changed into their fine clothing, stuffing their own lice-ridden rags under a log. As they mounted the men's horses, Dimitri said, "So, we go to West Coast?"

"East," Sasha said.

They glowered at each other until the sound of distant hoofbeats rose above the singing birds. Dimitri gnashed his teeth.

"Bah, to hell with you! Enjoy your filthy, cold East Coast. I go to West."

Sasha wheeled his horse in the opposite direction.

"And you enjoy that Spanish architecture, you ass. Goodbye."

Sasha did settle on the East Coast—in New York City—and since Natalia descended from him, what became of Dimitri was a mystery for over a century.

But that answer would come later. In the meantime, as Natalia approached Jacob on that breezy Martha's Vineyard beach, with her surreally titian hair fluttering and her blouse billowing so Jacob could see her emerald bikini top against her creamy skin, he knew he had found his Betsy. Sashaying towards him, Natalia smiled like a woman playing Cupid. When they were ten feet apart he sidestepped to walk around her and started to say "Good morning" when she stopped dead in front of him. She put a hand on her hip and shielded her eyes against the sun with the other.

"You're Jacob Stanley."

Admittedly he was taken by her shape, the sinuous flow of her body's lines, but what most entranced him— even *he* couldn't believe it—was her nose. So perfect, one could check a ruler's straightness by it.

"Yes, I'm Jacob."

"*You* are a genius."

He considered saying what Wyeth had to him— "*Gosh, you really think so?*"—but it wasn't in him to reply sarcastically to people's compliments, especially when the person giving the compliment made his mouth dry.

She playfully punched him in the stomach. "*You* need to paint me."

"That would be great." He swallowed. "When did you have in mind?"

"How about right now?"

"All...all right."

At some point on the way back, Natalia slipped under his arm. He made no attempt to separate the two of them. Nothing had ever felt so right, so comfortable.

He did paint Natalia—many times, including the scandalous *Natalia, Bound*, an arresting nude of a saucy Natalia, reclined on a beach, propped up on her elbow, entwined in thick nautical rope, with her hair and twisted strands of kelp tangled over her shoulders and breasts.

"Why, he's covered up the best parts," Wyeth said to Natalia when he viewed it. "My dear," he whispered in her ear, "you must let *me* paint you."

Natalia worked her lips like she was creasing lipstick, a facial "um" she used when formulating her thoughts.

"Andy," she said, "you have your Siri and your Helga and the young woman you're working on now, whoever she is. I am *Jacob's* Helga, and no one else's."

Wyeth scowled, shook a fist and stomped away.

Despite being denied Natalia as a model, when Natalia and Jacob were married, Wyeth graciously hosted the ceremony on his and Betsy's oceanside estate. It was a stunning July afternoon, 75 degrees and cloudless. For their honeymoon, reconciled to Jacob's predisposition to illness outside of New England, they went to Newport for two weeks, staying in the beach house of a patron of Wyeth's. Natalia would have preferred Hawaii or Fiji, two places she hadn't been, and though she secretly wondered if Jacob's falling ill outside of New England was a fabrication designed to narrow and therefore control his world, she tolerated it as the quirk of a great artist. Unable to travel to exotic places, she at least made sure they spent time in different areas of the region during each area's peak: summers in Maine, early autumn in the White Mountains, mid-autumn in Vermont, Thanksgiving in New Hampshire with his parents, Christmas in Boston with hers, skiing in Stowe, and springtime biking around Connecticut, Rhode Island and the Cape.

Yet despite Natalia's efforts to keep New England fresh for Jacob and his painting, 15 years after they were married an inexplicable discontent settled over him. Suddenly everything was too familiar. There wasn't a way that the New England light struck a barn that he hadn't seen. The smells that had once made him joyful and expansive—the first hints of salt air when driving north on Route 1 along the Maine coast; the intermingling of tanned moccasins and aged cheddar cheese in a Vermont general store; the aroma of fresh ale in a Boston brewpub; and while crossing the Connecticut River on a two-car ferryboat in the midsummer gloaming, the languid, muddy smell of life a hundred years ago—these same smells were stale and depressing to him now, bitter reminders of how little he'd seen of the world, as well as the bizarre ailment that forced him to stay put.

Sounds, too, deflated him. Whether the surf crashing on the rocks in Cutler, the train clanging into Waterbury station, or the antediluvian stillness of the woods around Walden Pond on a weekday afternoon, all pleasing sounds now ceased to refill his creative well. Even Natalia's lovely face failed to inspire him. After endless series in which Jacob strove to capture the rarified quality of her profile, not to mention the seductive expressiveness of her lithe wrists and slender hands, he felt himself suddenly empty, with nothing left to say about her. His painting dried up.

And then Natalia received an extraordinary email that she almost trashed because it opened like a plea from a former African finance minister in exile: "Dear Mrs. Stanley: Please forgive my intrusion, but I am the lawyer of a man named Anton Komissarzhevkaya, who has graciously asked that I contact you." She decided to call him back.

The lawyer said that Anton was the descendant of Dimitri K., who had always wanted to reconcile with his brother—especially after he struck gold and bought a huge tract of land in Northern California. Dimitri's will decreed that if the West Coast Komissarzhevkayas ever were without an heir, the estate should pass to the closest relative in the East. As an only child, and with her father recently dead, Natalia was that relative. Anton, although still alive, was dying of cancer and wanted to meet the person who would get his walnut ranch and vineyard. Could she come out immediately? Natalia replied that she would discuss it with her husband and get back to him.

Jacob wasn't in his studio. Instead she found him in the crow's nest he'd had built at the top of a tall oak. Climbing the long rope ladder to reach him, Natalia kept her eyes on the rung above and didn't look down. She rarely came up here—a shame because the view of Maple Juice Cove and the ocean beyond was spectacular. Far in the distance, at the mouth of the cove, a cruising yawl headed out to sea. There was a chill breeze coming off the water. Natalia took hold of Jacob's arms and made him cover her like a blanket.

"I have news." She explained the offer.

"Jesus," he said. "Two thousand acres? In California?"

"Incredible, right?"

"What about my...you know...?"

"I was thinking about that."

They would treat this first visit as a vacation, she said. No commitments. If Jacob got sick, when Natalia inherited they'd sell the place and stay in the East. But if by some miracle he didn't get sick, they'd consider keeping the place and running the business.

"But seriously, Natalia—a *nut farm*? We don't know anything about that stuff."

"And grapes, Jacob. Anyway, that's why Anton wants us out there—so he can show us the ropes."

Jacob studied the water. In the mid-afternoon light, it was an iridescent plane of color: Ultramarine, Dark Cerulean, Viridian and gunmetal, with hints of Feldgrau, gold, Salmon and even Burnt Sienna. Many factors affected the color of a body of water: depth, temperature, wind and time of day being just a few. Seascapes were not easy.

Still, Jacob had painted them forever, and he couldn't help wondering how his work might be reborn by moving to a strange place, like Gauguin's had when the Frenchman left Europe for the South Pacific. Before that he had been just another Postimpressionist, but after the move, when he started painting those native figures and tropical landscapes, Gauguin flourished. Maybe if Jacob did something equally radical (short of leaving Natalia, whom he adored), he would reach his highest potential, too. Staying in New England and in Wyeth's shadow might prevent him from ever finding his true voice as an artist. First, however, he had to see if he could be away from New England without falling ill.

"All right," he said, "set it up."

She smiled at him. Her hair blew across his face. She brushed it away.

"When should we leave?" she asked.

"Well, it sounds like your relative isn't long for this world. How about tomorrow?"

Which they did, and although he didn't feel sick during the flight or when they landed, by the time they were 50 miles north of Sacramento he began to have second thoughts.

"This is a ranch?" he asked.

"Yes."

Natalia drove with hands on the wheel at precisely 10 and 2 o'clock. Jacob liked having her drive. It allowed him to gaze out at the passing scenery, in this case gilded hills—an alien sight to a guy who had always associated high summer with green.

"So, it probably has dogs, right?" he said.

"It's a ranch, so, yes, I imagine there are dogs."

He groaned. One dog—one clean, quiet and well-behaved dog—Jacob could handle. But the dogs he had seen on New England farms—barking, slobbering, leaping dogs—were another matter. He loathed them, the smelly beggars.

"All right then." They passed a pear orchard and roadside farm stand. "For every smelly, barking dog we find when we get there, we take one day off the trip."

Natalia shrugged. "Okay, but I think you're being paranoid. It'll be fine. You'll see."

When they turned down the dusty driveway flanked by walnut trees, Jacob's immediate impression was how golden and dense the light was in this part of California. They passed a vineyard that grew down a modest slope, and when they rounded a bend, nine dirty mutts converged on the car from all directions.

"Crap," he said. "We're already in negative numbers."

Natalia laughed out loud.

They got out and stretched. The place was neater, more polished than Jacob had imagined; but then again his only picture of a California ranch was from Steinbeck's *Of Mice and Men*. He could feel the expansiveness of the place, except to the east, where a ridge loomed like a wall. Jacob was staring at it, wondering if there were mountain lions up there, when a screen door creaked open and banged shut and a big man stomped onto the porch. He wore a John Deere cap and faded denim overalls, his thumbs hooking the straps.

"Natalia?" he said.

"Yes. Anton?"

He came down the steps and lifted her in a bear hug two feet off the ground.

"So beautiful!" His eyes flashed around as if he expected to be contradicted. "Much more attractive than the California Komissarzhevkayas!"

"This is my husband, Jacob. Easy, Anton—he's a painter, he needs his hands."

Anton slapped Jacob's hand away and bear-hugged him, too. Jacob's first thought as the man heaved him off the ground and he smelled Aqua Velva on the man's neck was that Anton couldn't be as sick as his lawyer had led Natalia to believe.

He put Jacob down, nodded and boomed out, "Well…we'd better get the nuts in the car!"

He went to the porch in giant strides, grabbed a bulging burlap sack out of a rocking chair and slung it over his shoulder. Returning to them, he lifted the sack off his shoulder with such deceptive ease that, when Anton tossed it to him and Jacob caught it, it was like being pounced on by a lion. Jacob wheeled back ten feet before regaining his balance. By then Anton had his arm draped over Natalia's smooth shoulders and was strolling around, sweeping his free arm at the landscape. Jacob put the sack of walnuts in the trunk and hustled to catch up to him and Natalia. Meanwhile, he had no idea what they were supposed to do with all of those nuts.

During the two weeks they stayed on the ranch, Jacob kept bracing for some sudden illness to befall him, but it didn't happen. Although he felt a little more lethargic each day, that could be explained by the travel and the long days spent touring the ranch and the town of Sleeper.

The main house was a massive Victorian with a wide wraparound porch. Mornings Jacob liked to drink his coffee there, gazing at the seemingly endless rows of walnut trees. Afternoons Anton introduced them at the bank, town hall, cafe and VFW post, where they attended a barbecue fundraiser. Jacob and Natalia took a couple of sightseeing trips by themselves, to the redwoods, to the genteel coastal town of Mendocino, and to the northern coastal town of Arcata, where they ate pancakes at an old lumberjack cookhouse on a wooded peninsula that jutted into the Pacific. The setting reminded him vaguely of Roque Bluffs back in Maine.

It was all heady enough to make Jacob ignore the fact that, while he might not be ill, he *was* becoming increasingly tired with each passing day. Stimulated by the fresh vistas, he filled his pocket sketch book before they left and painted a pair of ranch scenes in watercolors for Anton.

As they lay in bed their last night on the ranch, Natalia finally broached the subject of their moving to Sleeper permanently.

"So what do you think? Could you do this?"

Jacob rolled over. "I'm not sure."

Moonlight streamed through the window, bathing her body in a milky glow. As if trying to sway him, she propped herself up on her elbow, like her pose in *Natalia, Bound*. Not a thread covered her.

"But you haven't felt sick, right?" she said.

"Tired, but not sick."

"So can I tell him we'll be back?"

"Sure," he said. "In a month."

Remarkably it only took half that time. Once they had packed and sent the moving company ahead with their belongings, all that was left to do was sell the tiny property—the cottage, converted barn studio and potting shed—a chore drastically simplified when Betsy Wyeth bought it for more than their asking price. The day before they were to leave, Wyeth wandered over and sat on the cottage steps with Jacob. The two drank wine from a wineskin he had brought. Jacob had never used one before and sprayed his shirt with Beaujolais. He passed the wineskin back.

"Sorry to see you go, kid," Wyeth said. "Just hope you know what the hell you're doing. When an artist finds his subject—the place and people that speak to him—he's taking a big risk walking away from that. Christ, what do you know about California? Don't tell me you fell in love with the place already."

"No, but I've been pretty dried up here. I don't see how it can hurt."

"Tell you what you do," Wyeth said. "Wait for this Russkie relative of hers to kick off, then sell the spread and high-tail it back here, where you belong. *California*"—he spat in disgust—"all that stucco and clay tile roofs and no damn seasons. How's a person live without seasons? I think you're going to miss it here, kid. You think all you want is that warm weather, but October comes and there's no color, and February comes and you're not up to your crotch in snow, you're going to start pining away for old New England. I'll bet all my brushes on it."

"You may be right," Jacob said, "but I have to find out for myself."

"That you do." Wyeth stood up and took the wineskin away from him. "Ought to make you go wring out that shirt, give me my wine back." They shook hands. "Take care of yourself, Jacob."

"You, too, Mr. Wyeth. Thank you for everything."

"Keep painting." The old man crossed the lawn and faded down the gravel drive.

The second time out to Sleeper, the lethargy struck Jacob much more suddenly. He was walking in a dry creek bed on the far side of the ranch when he suddenly felt lightheaded and his knees buckled. When he came to, it was dusk. A coyote was staring at him from the scrubby bank. Jacob got unsteadily to his feet, threw a rock at it, and watched it slink off through the orchard.

He didn't tell Natalia about the incident. She was having such a good time learning about the business and supervising the construction of Jacob's new studio, and he didn't want to spoil her fun. But when she saw him struggle to get out of bed morning after morning, when she saw him take ten minutes to walk a distance that should have taken him five, and when she saw him climb the stairs in the house and sweat from the exertion, Natalia knew he wasn't well.

"You say you're not sick," she said in the Safeway frozen foods section, "but I want you to see some doctors, just in case. We'll go down to San Francisco, make a little vacation of it. What do you say?"

"I've always wanted to see Alcatraz."

"Done." She shook a box of frozen spinach at him and tossed it in the cart.

After appointments with two specialists they took a tour boat over to the island in a dense fog. Once inside the prison, while Natalia stuck with the tour group, Jacob wandered off by himself to get his own sense of the place.

There was a palpable sense of despair on this hunk of rock in the middle of San Francisco Bay. The tiers of cells—evilly lit, no privacy, surrounded by a cavernous space—were crushing in their uniformity. Jacob noted the 70-foot climb to the roof, through tight wall spaces, handling steam pipes. Even with such obstacles, if Jacob had been stuck in here like Frank Lee Morris and his accomplices, he probably would have tried to escape, too.

He went outside and down a narrow staircase to the exercise yard. Seagulls, menacingly still, covered the concrete. They parted away from him as he followed another set of stairs down to the landing. The fog was breaking. Behind him gulls filled in the path he'd made, covering the entire hillside to the main building. Jacob's legs felt weak. He prayed he didn't collapse.

The fog had cleared enough to see the city across the Bay. Looking at the distance, remembering his own swimming between Penobscot Bay islands, and knowing how quickly cold water drained your energy, Jacob knew that Morris and the others had drowned. Motivation and adrenaline wouldn't have made a difference. Darkness, currents, cramps and sharks would have taken them. People romanticized to the contrary, but there were some places a person simply couldn't escape from. And if those men—tough, vigorous men who had planned their escape for months—couldn't get across a mile of water to freedom, what made him think that he, dog-tired and dragging, could get 3,000 miles away from New England? It was ridiculous. He turned from the water and started up the long concrete stairs, and as the gulls flapped away from him, he knew he was soon going to die.

Umpteen tests in San Francisco and Sacramento shed no light on his ever-worsening fatigue. In fact the tests only confused the doctors because they indicated he was in perfect health. Yet stairs and short walks—never mind strenuous exercise—drained him to the point that he required three naps a day. One hypothesis was mercury poisoning, but it was proved false like all the others. Exasperated, the doctors sent him home with prescriptions for an antidepressant and a mild stimulant.

Jacob knew that if he asked her to, Natalia would give up her inheritance and move back to New England, but he couldn't bring himself to do it. Her love of California and the warm, mild weather was obvious. He couldn't steal her joy. Besides, it comforted him to know that Natalia wouldn't have to worry about money when he was gone. After a decade of strong sales, Jacob's work had declined in popularity. He now made a modest income. And because Natalia had given up her own career to promote Jacob and make a home for them, she had no means of supporting herself. The walnut ranch and vineyard were essential to Natalia's future.

One day, Natalia announced, "If we can't be in New England, we'll bring New England to us." Overnight, she introduced elements of home to their life in California: lobsters and fresh-frozen blueberries from Maine; maple syrup from Vermont and New Hampshire; clam chowder from Legal Seafoods in Boston. A truckload of Poland Spring water was specially shipped as well. And when the Red Sox were on their West Coast swing, Natalia snagged much-coveted tickets to their games against the Oakland A's.

For a few months, it looked as if Natalia's tricks were working, but there was one thing she couldn't give him, something he could only get in New England itself: the seasons. Wyeth had been right. When October came, Jacob missed his meandering walks through the woods with the sour smell of leaf tannin in his nose. He missed the contrast of staggering in from a blizzard to a fire in the wood stove and an aproned Natalia at the oven. He missed the crackle of ice-caked branches warming in the sun. He missed the dramatic rebirth of spring and even the staggering heat and humidity of August. And he even missed that one chill day in early September that signaled the end of summer. California, on the other hand, was nothing *but* summer.

His nostalgia for New England spiked when he got a glimpse of California's dark side. First the state forest over the ridge burned for a week, shrouding the entire town in smoke. Then, one morning in January he was awakened by the headboard rattling against the wall. "Nothing to worry about," Anton said at their door. "Only a four-point-something. Happens again, try to get outside, or in a doorjamb." Jacob was not comforted.

Then Jacob learned—from the TV, which annoyed him—that Wyeth had died and the funeral was being held in Chadds Ford, Pennsylvania. He hadn't been invited, but even if he had, Pennsylvania wouldn't offer him any respite from the nagging fatigue; it had to be New England.

Anton was admitted to the hospital on a Tuesday morning in March and died that Saturday. Natalia, Jacob, and dozens of ranch hands and townspeople attended his church service, and most were at the family plot for his burial in the rain. Driving back to the house afterwards, Natalia looked at Jacob and started to cry.

"What's wrong?" he said.

"We should have gone back months ago. You can barely walk. Enough is enough, Jacob. We're leaving tomorrow."

"What about the place?" he asked.

"We'll sell it. I miss New England, too, Jacob."

It was the truth. Natalia missed haddock chowder at Cappy's in Camden, Maine. She missed the summer evening concerts on village greens all over Vermont. She missed the Narragansett beaches, the White Mountains, and the storied Boston campuses (including her own *alma mater*). She booked them on the first flight out of Sacramento the next morning and hastily packed their bags. In a few weeks, she'd return alone to sell the place and have their things moved back. For now, like Jacob, Natalia just wanted to go home.

It had rained for three days straight—the most rain she'd seen since they moved out here—and was still raining at four o'clock in the morning as she drove them south towards the airport. She rounded a corner and her headlights fell upon a massive hill of rock, brush and mud. The road had disappeared. It was as though an entire mountain had melted.

"Seems California doesn't want me to leave," Jacob said.

"To hell with that," Natalia said. "I'll get us out of here."

She turned around and sped north, then towards the coast to loop around the trouble, but encountered another mudslide in the hills. She tried going farther east, to wend south to Sacramento through wine country, and almost drove into a yawning sinkhole. There was no way out.

"We're going to miss our flight anyway," Jacob said. "Let's just go back."

Rain was gushing off the eaves when they pulled in front of the ranch house. Natalia tucked Jacob in on the living room sofa and lit a fire in the fireplace.

"There," she said. "This is sort of like home, right? I'll call up and change our flights to the weekend. They'll clear those mudslides by then, I'm sure. How about some blueberry pancakes and maple syrup to cheer you up?"

"I'd like that." He gave her fingers a weak squeeze, then reached up and traced the bridge of her nose. A nose even Helen of Troy would be jealous of. "My gorgeous Natalia. My greatest subject. My Helga, my *Madame X,* my—"

"Shh, quiet now." She smoothed his hair. "I'm glad I strong-armed you on the beach that day."

"What? I was the one—"

She kissed him and went into the kitchen. She was humming something, moving pans around. Jacob stared at the fire, then at one of his paintings hanging over the mantle: *Port Clyde, Sunrise.* Closing his eyes, he saw the glassy stillness of the water, the lobster buoys hanging from the side of a weatherbeaten shed, the sun glaring fiercely over the horizon. His breathing slowed.

Damn, those sunrises were blinding, no two ways about it.

The light grew brighter and brighter until it was no longer blinding at all.

ABOUT THE AUTHOR

Chris Orcutt has written professionally for over 20 years as a fiction writer, journalist, scriptwriter, playwright, technical writer and speechwriter.

Orcutt is the creator of the critically acclaimed Dakota Stevens Mystery Series, including *A Real Piece of Work* (#1), *The Rich Are Different* (#2) and *A Truth Stranger Than Fiction* (#3). Orcutt's short story collection, *The Man, The Myth, The Legend*, was voted by IndieReader as one of the best books of 2013. And his modern pastoral novel *One Hundred Miles from Manhattan* (an IndieReader Best Book for 2014) prompted *Kirkus Reviews* to favorably compare Orcutt to Pulitzer Prize-winning author John Cheever.

As a newspaper reporter Orcutt received a New York Press Association award, and while an adjunct lecturer in writing for the City University of New York, he received the Distinguished Teaching Award.

If you would like to contact Chris, you can email him at corcutt007@yahoo.com or tweet him @chrisorcutt. For more information about Orcutt and his writing, or to follow his blog, visit his website: www.orcutt.net.

Excerpt from
One Hundred Miles from Manhattan

This is a novel about an wealthy rural community—Wellington, NY—where the hills and the seemingly quaint village conceal lives of love, lust, adultery, tragedy and small wars. Unlike other novels in the pastoral tradition, which often tell the story of a place and a time through the eyes of a single character, this modern novel uses 10 narrators to shed light on this exclusive community. Following is the opening of the novel.

Until that early June evening in bed beside her much older husband, Caprice Highgate had never heard the screams of terrified cows. In fact, before moving upstate from Manhattan to Wellington she hadn't heard so much as a *moo* out of one. Even after three years, on nights like this she longed for the white noise of the city. The sustained silence of the country was deafening, and when there *was* noise, like now with the wailing cows and the howling coyotes, it more than startled her—it shredded her nerves. She waved a hand at the open windows.

"I wish you'd do something about that."

Hamilton was reading an armchair safari book: Robert Ruark's *Use Enough Gun*. He turned a page. Caprice glanced at the double-barreled shotgun hanging over the bedroom door.

"Maybe try *using* a gun instead of reading about them," she said. "Did you hear me?"

"What?"

"Your cows. There are coyotes out there, Hamilton. Hear them?"

"Coyotes?"

"Well, they're not wolves."

"Stephen's on top of it, I'm sure," he said. "Take a pill."

"That's your answer—take a pill."

"Caprice, don't be melodramatic."

She put on her robe and went downstairs.

She poured herself a glass of wine, padded into the great room, opened the French doors and sat in an armchair facing outside. For a minute it was pin-quiet, but then another burst of the melee shattered the silence: the calves' bleats for help, followed by the coyotes' eerie whistles. She sipped some wine and gazed out into the darkness. Half a mile away, Celia's bedroom lights glared across the long, narrow pond (a moat, really) in front of the mansion. Caprice wondered how the first Mrs. Highgate was faring and whether the carnage was keeping her awake, too. She hoped so. She hoped the bitch died from sleep deprivation so she and Hamilton could move into the mansion. This place had always felt like a child's playhouse by comparison.

In the morning after coffee, Caprice dressed in riding clothes and Wellies, got in her Range Rover and drove to the stables. One of the hands must have seen her coming because when Caprice got inside, Giorgio was already out of his stall with the saddle pad on his back. The air was thick with hay dust. She sneezed.

"Bless you," the stable hand said.

"Thanks. Stephen around?"

"Office, Miss Caprice."

She changed into her riding boots, grabbed her crop and helmet, and marched into the office. Stephen was on the phone. He raised a finger to her.

Caprice stood at the window and pretended to watch Giorgio being walked out to the yard. Instead, in the reflection she watched Stephen trace the curve of her backside. Caprice knew her ass was good, but the breeches helped.

"Miss Caprice," Stephen said, hanging up the phone. "What can I do you for?"

She fastened her helmet strap. "Have you *heard* the cows at night, Stephen?"

"Heard what?"

"You're as bad as Hamilton. Don't tell me you haven't noticed. The cows, the coyotes."

"Coyotes? *No*...they're not big enough to go after cattle."

She stared at him. "So you think I'm hearing things."

"No, it's just—"

"Saddle up, Stephen. We're going riding."

"Where?"

"Wherever the cows are."

He leaned back in his chair. "That won't be so easy, Miss Caprice."

Stephen launched into a monologue about Hamilton's 200 head of cattle being spread across all 2,500 acres of the estate. Since the animals wandered freely spring through fall, the noises Caprice heard—*if* she'd heard them—could have come from anywhere. As the estate manager, he knew about these things.

"Humor me then," she said.

"You're the boss." Stephen grabbed a rifle from behind his chair.

"What's that for?"

"In case you're right."

They rode all morning, scouring patchworks of fields separated by dense hedgerows. The weather was clear, affording a beautiful view of the Village of Wellington and the endlessly undulating, tree-dappled hills. They also saw a lot of Hamilton's cattle—Black Angus, Stephen informed her—as they searched for signs of the violence that had kept her awake last night.

As the noon fire horn carried faintly from the village, Stephen pulled up beneath the ancient oak that sheltered the Highgate family cemetery. The earliest stone dated back to 1711. Tiger lilies grew wild along the picket fence. Caprice loathed coming to this spot on the estate; headstones awaited Hamilton and Celia, but there was no space earmarked for her...